Found by the Road

BOOKS BY DALE E. LEHMAN

HOWARD COUNTY MYSTERIES

The Fibonacci Murders
True Death
Ice on the Bay
A Day for Bones

BERNARD AND MELODY CAPERS

Weasel Words

OTHER NOVELS

Space Operatic

SHORT STORY COLLECTIONS

The Realm of Tiny Giants
Found by the Road

FOUND

BY THE

ROAD

stories by
DALE E. LEHMAN

RED TALES

Chase, Maryland

Found by the Road
Dale E. Lehman

Copyright © 2022 by Dale E. Lehman

All rights reserved. Except as permitted under U.S. Copyright Act of 1976, no part of this publication may be reproduced, distributed, or transmitted in any form or by any means, or stored in a database or retrieval system, without the prior written permission of the publisher.

This is a work of fiction. All the characters, organizations, and events portrayed in this book are either products of the author's imagination or are used fictitiously.

Cover art by Proi

Book design by Dale E. Lehman
Book set in 11-pt. Le Monde Livre Classique

Published by Red Tales, 2022
Baltimore, Maryland
United States of America
https://www.DaleELehman.com

Trade paperback: 978-1-958906-02-6
Ebook: 978-1-958906-03-3

Dedication

For Geoffrey, a superhero of a different sort.

THE STORIES

Grandpa Becker's Second-Hand Time Machine	11
The Winter Thief	17
Road Trip	24
Lesson	33
Woodsmoke	34
Dust	37
The Bamboo Carrier	38
For Emergency Use Only	44
Angry Bird	48
Adoption	49
Reunion	68
Falling Man	72
Bird Feeder	78
In Plain Sight	86
Olly Olly Oxen Free!	89
Count to Ten	91
Christmas Future	97
Fireworks at Midnight	101
Rush, Rush, Rush	106
Entanglement	110
Stuck	119
Do Not Open	123
How Not to Camp	131
Thirty Minutes of Evil	132
The Boss	141
Down by Two	147
The End of Everything	148
The Case of the Drive-Thru Cheeseburger	153
The Ghost in the Stacks	156
Not Quite a Ghost Story	161
Goldenrod is Here	167

Introduction

The stories collected here were born in a happier time, from December 2018 ("Christmas Future") through September 2020 ("Adoption")—in other words, from pre-COVID through lockdown. You might not remember lockdown as a happy time, but I do. Relieved of the need to commute to work, I largely spent my days at home with my wife Kathleen, oblivious that two years later she would succumb to liver disease, leaving me on my own for the first time in my adult life. I wish those days could have lasted forever.

But let's talk about the stories.

As with my first collection, *The Realm of Tiny Giants*, this is an eclectic mix of genres including flash fiction and longer tales, award-winners and stories I just plain like. It's hard for me to pick a favorite. The first roadside find is "Grandpa Becker's Second-Hand Time Machine," which I wrote for a contest by Medium.com publication *Don't Wake the Mage*, where it garnered an honorable mention. "The Winter Thief" was just plain fun to write, while "Road Trip" might be my best science fiction story yet.

Okay, stop. I've only covered the first three. Let's cast our gaze into the middle distance.

A quarter mile or so down the road, a special pair of stories await: "Adoption" and "Reunion." These deal with a notorious space pirate and her adopted "son." I created the characters in the 1990s and only returned to them during the pandemic when invited to submit a story to a collection titled *Writers in Lockdown*. It seemed a good time to revisit their relationship. "Adoption" tells how they first came together, and "Reunion" (written for *Lit Up* on Medium.com) explores how they grew apart yet remained bound. Their original story, along with a snippet from a possible novel, slumbers in my files. I hope to write more about them someday.

Halfway along the road, you'll find four holiday tales: "Olly Olly Oxen Free!" and "Count to Ten" for Halloween, "Christmas Future" for (obviously) Christmas, and "Fireworks at Midnight" for New Year's Eve. The first three are just for fun, the last a bit more serious, not to mention it showcases my interest in astronomy.

Keep traveling, and you'll encounter "Rush, Rush, Rush," one of the very few romance tales I've written. There's a story behind that story. Written for the NYC Midnight Short Story Contest, "Rush, Rush, Rush" wasn't completed in time for entry because, as luck had it, we were moving to a new home that weekend. My first story for the contest, "Hot Ice," put me in the top five of my section, so I had high hopes of advancing to the second round. Then the deadline clobbered me in the face. Ouch! So much for that contest. (I didn't include "Hot Ice" here. It will likely appear in my next collection.)

One final note. "The Ghost in the Stacks" tells of a specter haunting a public library and a young lady who befriends him. This is a not-so-subtle nod to my favorite writer, the late, great Ray Bradbury. I hope he likes it and maybe assures Kathleen she did a pretty good job mentoring me over all those decades.

It may be a mistake to mix genres with such wild abandon, but let's be honest. A good story is a good story no matter its time or place, no matter its subject. And I did pick these because (if I do say so myself) I think they're good. So don't think about genres. Just get comfortable, relax, and hit the accelerator.

Enjoy the drive!

Grandpa Becker's Second-Hand Time Machine

(Don't Wake the Mage Honorable Mention)

Memory is a liar.

That's what I told Holly later that night. With our three young children in tow, we were driving cross-country to my grandfather's southern Illinois farmhouse. Our route skirted my hometown, so as a treat for my family—or myself, at least—we detoured to revisit my parents' old homestead. Talk about a rude awakening.

The flickering film of my memory records a sprawling, beige ranch with dark brown trim, a huge yard lined with flower beds, a massive vegetable garden in back that I help my father tend each summer, a back yard corralled by a rail fence bristling with splinters, and a giant green swing set a kid can pump high enough to kick the moon. Our neighbor's house to the right presents a huge, white façade fronted by a mile-long porch where I stand with adults towering over me while a partial eclipse of the sun darkens the world. Two doors the other direction, a gray old mansion overhung by enormous trees lurks in perpetual shade. Ghosts haunt it while, up and down the street, children jump rope and run and laugh in the sun.

Now, forty years later, I found houses shrunk with age and the neighbor's porch chipped down to a slab a few paces long. The children had run off, taking the ghosts with them. Most of the flowerbeds had died, or maybe they'd been dug up. Only the roads flowed and bent as I remembered. Otherwise, the neighborhood's character had blown away like vapor on the wind.

That night in our hotel room, after the kids had fallen asleep, I lay awake, replaying memories, wondering where that world had gone. "I guess I'm old," I whispered to Holly.

She snuggled close and purred, "Sure are. High side of fifty."
"What happened?"
"Time, Frank. Just time."
"Then I need a time machine."
That amused her. "You need sleep. Long drive tomorrow."

Unlike me, Grandpa Becker still lived in the house where he grew up, a white two-story farmhouse with a curving gravel drive, a massive red barn, and a white garage big enough for five cars, now empty of vehicles. Uncle Jason, my father's oldest brother, and his wife Aunt Sally lived with Grandpa. Ancient specters had already possessed the farm when I was young. They shadowed us in those days, my cousins and I, leading us on as we stomped between rows of corn, climbed ladders in the barn, hunted Easter eggs in the yard. And still they hung about, not having aged a day, longing to play with a new generation of youth.

We arrived at suppertime. Aunt Sally had a pot roast waiting, and after dinner and the inevitable stampede of children through house and yard, the young ones were packed off to bed so the old folks could talk around the kitchen table. An hour later, Grandpa Becker pulled himself to his feet and, walker firmly in hand, hobbled to the living room. Holly stayed in the kitchen with my aunt and uncle while I followed to the well-worn tan sofa in the cramped living room. We sat in silence for a time while the ticking of the old clock on the wall measured the rise and fall of voices from the kitchen.

"Feeling your joints today," Grandpa commented. "Aren't you?"

I told him of our detour, the lies of memory, how the traces of yesterday had wandered off, leaving me no present and maybe no future. "You're lucky," I said. "You still have your ghosts all around you all the time."

He smiled his toothy smile and pushed up his wire-rim glasses on his wrinkled face. At ninety-seven, his mind was still as sharp as a katana blade, although his body might snap in two at any moment. "What you need, Frank, is a time machine."

"That's what I told Holly."

"You're your grandfather's grandson for sure."

"Have you invented one?"

"No, but I came by one." He gave me an impish grin.

I was willing to play along. His games always proved amusing. "Where?"

"At the flea market. Come on, I'll show you."

He extended a thin arm and reached for me with shaking fingers. I rose and helped him up. Forsaking his walker, he clung to my arm as we made our way to the back of the house, where an abandoned bedroom now served as a holding pen for the stash of curios he'd bought at garage sales and second hand stores over the past fifteen years. If Grandma Becker were still alive, she wouldn't have indulged him so, but he had no one to overrule him since her passing and little else on which to spend his money. And so he collected, stashed, and probably forgot all manner of other people's cast-offs.

It was a well-organized junk room, filled with metal racks stuffed with the broken and unidentifiable. Power cords dangled here, plastic doll eyes gazed out there. An ornately carved object with a stretched, tetrahedral head and curved grip caught my eye. He tapped it as we passed by. "Maori war club. Got it from the son of a World War II sailor. Here we go."

His shaking fingers brushed over a black box with a dark lens in one end and a white wheel mounted in a groove on the side. "Take this," he commanded, "and this box here." The plain cardboard box, its flaps tucked shut, was twice the size of the projector.

I had a time carting box, projector, and grandfather back to the living room. Once seated, he tugged at the box flaps. "Have a look inside."

Little white cardboard squares filled it, each a frame securing a slip of film. I took one out and held it up to the light. A beach scene, I thought, although details were hard to make out.

"It's a slide projector," he explained. "You put those slides into the carousel, turn on the light, and project the images onto a white screen. I don't have a screen, but the wall will do."

Holly slipped into the room. "Your aunt and uncle are off to dreamland," she said, eying the contraption. "Where are you two going?"

"I'm for bed myself," Grandpa told her. "You youngsters should take a jaunt through the past." He rummaged in the box for a moment and handed me another slide. Grabbing his walker, he wrestled himself to his feet and with a wink left us alone.

"Who's past is that?" Holly asked.

Holding the slide up to the light, I found it to be blank. "Good question."

"What are they, family vacations from a thousand years ago?"

"Not our family's. Grandpa bought this off somebody."

"Great. Let's hope they gave away something embarrassing, at least."

We set up the machine, doused the lights, and started the show. Projected on the white wall, a sequence of mundane images paraded before our eyes. Families frolicking on a public beach. Old folks seated around dinner tables. Parents helping toddlers unwrap presents around a Christmas tree. Swimsuited kids skipping through a lawn sprinkler and swinging on swings. Nothing out of the ordinary, nothing embarrassing, and certainly nothing to do with us, except maybe to spark our own memories. They reminded me what a liar memory was, but as they paraded by, I realized why. The house, the yard, the neighbor's porch, the haunted mansion, they had all been measured and recorded by a child's eyes, not an adult's. Back then, I stood at the foot of the mountain looking up. Now, nearing the summit, the view had changed.

I slid the blank slide into the machine. The featureless splash of light on the wall provided a fitting denouement to the show.

Until Holly leaned forward and asked, "What's *that*?"

Almost imperceptibly, the light spread. It crept along the wall, up and down, right and left, out even into the air, stealing closer and closer, while at its heart something happened, something like the skin of an apple being peeled away, something like the gray film on a lottery ticket being scratched off in fevered anticipation, and from within something peeked out. We found ourselves looking through a rip in the light, a rent in space, an incision in time. We found ourselves looking at...

...*us*.

Our fifty-plus selves looked back on our twentyish selves looking forward and found the younger couple full of optimism, full of themselves.

"A big old house," young Holly was saying, "with a fireplace and a lot of land."

"Five acres at least," the young me replied. "Forested. Secluded. Perfect for writing."

I knew his thoughts and feelings, saw through his eyes, heard with his ears. We or they or all of us at once sat at a small kitchen table in a tiny apartment, she doodling in a notebook, he leafing through a *National Geographic*. She turned the notebook so he could see what she'd drawn. "Something like this for the writing room. My desk here, yours here, the middle for both of us, so we can collaborate. Or whatever." She winked.

"Where do we build?" he asked, and as one all four of us answered, "In the mountains."

She laughed, and on and on they or we planned, oblivious to reality, building a private city in the clouds, believing every word of it, never doubting it would come to pass.

"I remember that day," Holly, my Holly, older and wiser Holly, said.

So did I, and this time memory matched reality, if reality this was, this fracture in time courtesy of a blank scrap of film. How could *that* be? But the vision floated before our eyes, product of a real, honest-to-God time machine even though it didn't transport our bodies anywhere in time.

She reached forward and clicked off the projector. The rip healed and the light vanished, returning us to Grandpa Becker's old living room in the ancient farmhouse.

"It didn't quite turn out like that," Holly commented. She smiled a small, faint smile, but not of regret.

It sure hadn't. We traded our dream home in the mountains for a common house in the suburbs. We still wrote on and off, but writing as a way of life yielded to more reliable employment. Children crowed into our private little world, expanding it beyond measure. Yes, our vision faded in the face of life, but maybe we'd traded up.

"We wouldn't be us if it had," I told her.

"Nor if we hadn't dreamed it." She rested her head on my shoulder. "That must have been a great place to be a kid. Your old neighborhood, I mean."

Indeed, it was. Exactly as I remembered it.

The Winter Thief

The snow gave him the idea. He squinted out the window at last season's corn stubble poking through the freeze. The snow, a blanket whiter than white sequined with fragments of sunlight, sparkled as he turned this way, that way, now left eye open, now right. The land reposed in death awaiting a vernal trumpet blast to call it from its sepulcher. But that was an age off and this the graveyard of January, the dark night of Gaia's soul.

Foley Granger, mug of steaming coffee in hand, blinked into the glare and wondered if the old lady even breathed. Surely, she must. Though this be the sleep of the dead, it wasn't death. She must once a day draw silent breath, then in the night's stone quiet release it unheard: in cold, out cold; in cold, out cold; until April when her eyelids fluttered and she sucked a long, cool gasp and exhaled warmth.

But now it was winter, and Foley was alone with Uncle Jim's farm and Uncle Jim's books and the snow. Uncle Jim and Aunt Sarah had flown south with the bobolinks. "Your aunt's grown allergic to the cold," Jim had said with that twisty smile of his. "From now on, we over-winter in the land of perpetual summer. I'll pay you to keep crooks and neighbors at bay while you do whatever it is you do."

"I write, Uncle Jim. You've got my books."

"All voodoo to me. You wave your hands over that computer and books come out."

Foley figured there was voodoo and there was voodoo. Uncle Jim conjured crops from dirt, didn't he?

But just now, magic had taken a vacation. January's freeze had overspread Earths' nicks and scratches with an elegant tablecloth. The dirt remained lifeless, while Foley hadn't written a word worth reading. He'd used the delete key more than the qwerties. He needed an idea.

And the snow had been there all along, awaiting his notice.

First, a disguise. A winter disguise like the snow, pure bright sparkling virginal to conceal his gloom. He bought it online, white and winter-ready: coat, snow pants, boots, gloves, ski mask. The items arrived in four shipments scattered over the breadth of a week, and when they were stacked in a pile, he stuffed himself into the garments. The old mirror at the end of the dim hall reflected an arctic soldier, or maybe a yeti.

Out into the snow he stomped, leaving craterlet footprints along the buried walk, up the concealed gravel drive to the barn, down the snow-covered dirt lane to the woods beyond. He was whiteness in a world of white accented by gray tree trunks, gray outbuildings, a leaden sky above, and shadows in the snow, small indentations of rabbit feet not yet erased by the wind. Striking across the field, Foley made elephant tracks into the heart of nowhere. He stumbled through furrows and tripped over stubble, an ungainly creature wrapped in faux fur, warm underneath, sweating in the cold. He reached the middle of the field, spread his arms, and flopped on his back. A snow angel explosion of powder puffed away on the wind.

Starting point marked, he clambered to his feet and traced out a spiral track, a minuscule circle followed by a tiny circle expanding into a small circle, turning, turning, ever outward, enlarging orbit by orbit by orbit as he traipsed not quite drunkenly around and around, gouging a crop circle devoid of crops. Nazca in the American Midwest. In the westward distance, the dark bulk of the Weisner farmhouse brooded; to the north, the faded red of the Mitchell barn; to the east, Uncle Jim's graying empire. Was anyone watching this white-on-white cyclone spinning at a crawl through the field, stirring up the snow? Probably not. But what might they think if they were? What would they see, what would they imagine?

What would old Weisner's daughter Hope think? Foley imagined her puzzled, frightened, intrigued, a blizzard of conflicting emotion swirling about her porcelain cheeks and rose lips. What *was* that thing out there? Man, machine, animal, spirit? An alien from the depths of space? Would she grab her father's arm, pry him from his couch, hobble him to the window to explain? What would *he* make of this strange vision? What stories would they spin?

Foley had but to imagine. He liked the alien angle. He was partial to aliens, and he'd never written about a snow-white alien stomping out crop circles in the cropless cold. Who, in fact, had?

Somewhere amid his circling and plotting, time wandered off for a sandwich. Cold seeped through the piled layers of his white cocoon and chilled his perspiration. He'd been out too long. In the northwest corner of the field where dark skeletons of slumbering oaks and maples overarched a creek, he paused to lean on a gnarled trunk and rest. His legs had about turned to stone and his breath clouded before his face. Enough of this. He had his story in vague outline. Time to get back to the warm, another cup of coffee, a sandwich, the tick of computer keys conjuring a tale about bleached aliens and the pale, frightened girl next door.

He took a step homeward.

Underfoot, snow slipped sideways and a chunk of frozen earth gave way. Foley spilled down the slope to the creek, broke through the ice, and took on water. It wasn't deep, only to his knees, but he fell laid out on his side, and it soaked him as sure as a tidal wave. He splashed about, regained his footing, and shaking from adrenaline and cold clawed up the slope on hands and knees, groping at low branches as he went.

Snow alien became ice sculpture. Stinging wind bit into his face and arms and legs. He could barely take a step, and the warmth of the house seemed five hundred miles off across the snow-crusted field.

I'm going to die, he thought. *I'm going to die in my uncle's field and won't be found until plowing begins in the spring.*

He forced his frozen legs to move, step by painful step, until some vaguely lucid part of his brain demanded he about-face. Uncle Jim's was too far, but he could make the Weisner place. Maybe.

Teeth chattering, arms clenching his torso, hands working with little success to rub warmth back into his chilled frame, he blundered to the property line and stumbled toward the house. Long before he arrived, a shadow moved behind the window, watching, waiting. As he clumped up the porch, the door opened, and a wave of heat washed over him. He recalled neither saying a word nor hearing a word nor seeing a face. He only knew someone helped him out of his sodden clothing, wrapped him in a blanket, and rested him on an old blue couch. More blankets piled on, and a mug of hot liquid came into his hands.

Lucidity seeped into his brain as the heat of the mug's contents trickled down his throat.

"Better?" Hope Wiesner asked.

He noticed her now, a woman his own age, early thirties, pretty of face, rough hands used to hard work in a way his weren't, dressed in blues and greens that reminded him of birdsong and tree buds opening and vernal flowers in the sun.

He nodded, embarrassed at being so stupid, so pathetic, so attracted.

"What on earth were you doing out there, blundering 'round and 'round in the snow?"

So she had seen. Had she thought of aliens, or only of dumb neighbors pulling idiot stunts in the cold? "Searching for ideas." He passed her the empty mug.

Hope vanished into the kitchen and returned with it full of hot cocoa. Was that what he'd been drinking? He supposed so. He sipped it, and it was good.

"Find any?" she asked. "Ideas?"

That wasn't what he expected her to say. She ought to have laughed in his face, told him what a fool he was. "One or two."

"Like what?"

"Winter aliens. Cropless crop circles. Frightened young women."

Hope settled into a ladder-back chair, crossed her legs at the ankles, crossed her arms over her chest. "Should I be worried that that almost makes sense?"

It seemed more polite to drink cocoa and say nothing, but eventually the refreshment ran out and she remained, watching and waiting. Foley wondered where old Mr. Weisner was.

"I suppose I should go." He began to rise but stopped when he realized he was wearing nothing but the blanket. He turned sunset red.

"They're in the dryer," she explained.

"All of them?"

Her arched eyebrow reminded Foley of the nurse who tended his broken arm years before. "You were soaked to the skin and freezing to death," she said. "What was I supposed to do?"

She had a point. But still, he was sitting naked under a blanket on her couch while her father lurked somewhere nearby. And she'd put him there.

"That's what you get," she laughed. "Trying to rob Old Man Winter, swirling around like one of his snowstorms, hoping to sneak up on him and steal his ideas. He plays for keeps."

Foley liked that image even better than white aliens. "What did you think when you saw me?" he asked.

"That you need more exercise."

He blushed. "Out in the snow, I mean."

"What do you think I thought? It's not every day you see some-body wandering aimlessly about a field in January. I figured you were a nutcase and would get yourself in trouble. You certainly got yourself in trouble. Are you a nutcase?"

"I'm a writer."

"Ah-ha. You *are*."

Foley blushed again.

She laughed. "I know whereof I speak. I'm a poet in my spare time."

Suddenly the pale winter sunlight, the warmth of the house and the cold beyond, the snow on the fields, the ice in the creek, even sit-ting before her in nothing but a blanket seemed right. "What kind of poetry?"

"Whatever comes to mind when I look out the window or walk to the barn or rescue sodden strangers at the door."

"Then you steal from the old fellow, too. You're also a winter thief."

"And spring, summer, and autumn," she agreed

"Can I read your poetry sometime?"

She hesitated.

"I'm watching my uncle's farm while he and my aunt sun them-selves down south," Foley said, pointing out the window. "I'll be here all winter, and I've nothing much to do but write."

Hope laughed. "And fall into frozen creeks."

"I'll try not to do that again."

"Good. 'Cause it actually wasn't much fun, stripping off all those cold, soggy garments." She winked at him.

He took a long drink so as not to meet her eyes.

"I'll make you a deal," she continued. "You can read mine if I can read yours."

"Deal," he agreed. He handed her the empty mug. Maybe Old Man Winter hadn't had the last laugh, after all.

She got him another refill and they sat, a pair of thieves sharing tales of past heists, until Foley's clothes were dry and she gave him privacy to dress and invited him to dinner.

Only once the table was laid did Mr. Weisner hobble in from somewhere in back, a funny smile on his wrinkled face. He said a blessing over the food and, with a wink at Foley, the same wink as his daughter's, added, "And while You're at it, keep an eye on these two filchers. Seems neither can stay out of trouble on their own. Amen."

Foley patted his yet-clean mouth with his napkin.

Hope smiled at him. "Dad hears like a bat."

"And devours pages like a bookworm," her father added. "Tell me about this snowbound alien, young man."

So he'd scored quite a haul for his troubles, Foley had. For the rest of that evening, it snowed stories and poems in Weisner's kitchen.

Road Trip

My vehicle crunched through the sulphur frost coating the mottled ground while inside the passenger compartment air circulators whirred and pinpricks of green light assured me all systems were nominal: temperature, atmosphere, the quantum shielding interposed between me and instant death.

I rode the programmed course alone, immersed in a world no human could touch. Outside, the frozen atmosphere clung to rock or steamed along the edges of cauldrons of searing magma while explosions launched liquid fire into orbit and beyond. Above this sterile land of reds and yellows and browns, five thousand stars shone cold and remote, their unfelt fire sprinkled liberally across the sky save in one great hole in the universe that swallowed the sun and its brethren.

An insane place for a road trip, this. But what a way to go!

To understand the end, return to the beginning, the year 2121, the year I was simultaneously created and betrayed. I mention the latter for context alone. I no longer seek to fix blame. For a man in my position, spite is pointless. For anyone, really. But as to why it happened, it's just this: some ages inherit an excess of moral confusion. That was such a time, when people seeking good did great evil without comprehending, while others, caring nothing for right and wrong, did as they pleased.

As to the facts, they run thus, insofar as I know them.

In that year, medical researchers tinkering with genetic switches thought they had cured death. Their success with microbes emboldened them to engineer immortal plants, then animals. Drunk on optimism or power or both, they rushed onward. Only later did they realize the cost of heeding the serpent in their Eden.

Of twenty human immortals grown in their lab, nineteen died within four years, ravaged by cancers. The same horror soon visited itself upon most of their altered plants and animals. A cure for cellular death, possibly, but complex organisms are more than the sum of their cells. The team scrambled to find salvation for their victims and themselves, but there was none. The one surviving immortal human was doomed to an eternity of cancer treatments. Finally, the researchers themselves became victims, disappeared with their records by the very government that had funded their work.

The one surviving immortal was hidden away, treated as ordinary, told nothing. But the bliss of ignorance couldn't last. At forty, possessed of the looks and stamina of a man half his age, he knew he was different, even without the bombardment of medical tests and treatments that was his lot.

That was two hundred seven years ago. I still don't look a day over thirty.

Physical immortality isn't bliss. Aside from the medical torture—individual cancers can be defeated, but they are legion, and nobody knows how to stop their ambushes—boredom is the chief enemy. In a normal lifetime, novelty hides under every rock. Double that span, triple it, bound it only by the lifetime of the universe, and you run out of rocks. At least, each looks so like those you've already turned that what's the point? Boredom sires apathy, depression, and eventually a terrible longing for the one thing nobody will let you have.

An end.

Avni Zelenya, my travel agent for the past forty-seven years, had heard that speech so often she wanted to vomit whenever I got that desperate look that preceded it. I'd met Avni when she was new on the job, twenty-three years old with skin as brown as a fresh-plowed field and a smile as bright as the sun. I was only one hundred ninety-three by the clock and in my mid-twenties by hormones and fancied we'd make a great couple. But she was already married then and at seventy still was, to the same man, so I grudgingly admit she made the right choice.

She chastised my whining before it could start. "Earth remains as big, and, no, you haven't seen everything. You've never once been to Greenland. Take a hiking tour of the remaining glaciers in the interior, for God's sake, before they're completely gone."

"I suppose," I agreed. "I might fall down a crevasse."

"Don't be stupid. Adventure guides don't lose clients."

"What if I want them to?"

"Ask someone else. I'm your friend."

"That's why I'm asking. I only need three things." I counted them on my fingers. "New. Spectacular. Deadly."

"Greenland *is* new and spectacular."

We'd performed this act *ad nauseum*, but this time it was different. The cancers and boredom, the apathy and depression were old enemies. A new foe had recently joined their ranks. Exhaustion. Paradoxically, the only way to defeat them all was to let them win.

My silence got to Avni. "I'm booking, whether you want it or not." Her fingers hovered over the display on her desktop, but she didn't do it, and I knew why. She wanted me to give the word, which I didn't. I felt sorry for her. I hadn't always been such a pain. I wished I didn't have to be now.

She leaned back, dropped her hands in her lap, wrestled down the agony of knowing me. "A space tour, then."

"I've done space."

"Shut up. You've only done the Apollo landing site tour." Her fingers danced over the desktop, calling up images that, with a flick of her wrist, she turned so I could see. "Rimworld Adventures. The only tour operating beyond Mars. They offer something other companies can't. Or won't."

On the electronic brochures, the lunar gray and the rusty sands of Mars flipped before my eyes, crossed by specialized vehicles transporting wide-eyed, wide-mouthed men, women, and children. I'd seen those eyes before, in person. That wasn't what Avni was selling. "Go on," I said.

"Jovian satellites." She flipped another set of brochures my way. "Ganymede." Flip. "Europa." Flip. "Callisto." Flip. "And for the ridiculously rich and insane, Io."

On her screen, lava lakes seethed as volcanoes spit magma into space.

This was what I'd come for. I could barely find my voice. "I thought you couldn't do deadly."

"I can't. Rimworld takes no chances. They built a special vehicle for Io, designed to withstand the radiation trapped in Jupiter's magnetic field. The surface is always changing, but they've done extensive geologic studies and use advanced AI to predict safe routes. They set you down, the vehicle takes you on a preprogrammed tour, and they pick you up at the end. Six hours, start to finish. Emergency evacuation plans are in place and tested regularly, but in seventeen tours over two years on Io, they've never had to use them." Avni leaned forward, looking for all the world like a prison guard about to take a club to me. "They aren't interested in blowing that record."

Of course, they weren't. I didn't care. "How much?"

"The package includes three months of training, transportation out and back, and the tour. It costs four years of your life and a mere ten million common."

Immortals have time. And money? Interest compounded over two hundred years generates a respectable stash. "I'll take it," I said.

The IoMobile—my name for the egg-shaped contraption rolling me across the yellowed surface of the tortured Jovian moon—could make fifteen kilometers an hour. I had limited ability to control it. I could to a degree speed up and slow down, stop to take in the view, and veer twenty meters to either side of the plotted course, but the nav system would wrest control if I gawked too long or meandered too much. Yet I didn't feel at its mercy. It carried me through an undulating land of solidified lava flows scarred by occasional depressions called patera, some dark and cold, some oozing fiery lava capped with newly formed black rock. The molten lakes slowly churned, pots boiling in slow motion. I stopped often, drawn into the spirit dance of red and yellow light.

Overhead, the black of Jupiter's night side blotted out the stars. Io's insides, spewed into space by volcanic eruptions, peppered its master's fierce radiation belts, sparking faint glimmers of auroras in the dark, distant cloud tops. I paused the vehicle at the crest of a rise to watch the sun glide over Jove's rim. Its warmth touched Io's surface, making the frozen sulfur atmosphere steam. Thin vapors swirled about me as the poisonous air reconstituted itself.

I'd spent too long ogling, in the IoMobile's estimation. It moved on despite my protests. A dark red glow grew on the horizon ahead. Beyond, a plume of fire jetted into the cosmos. The atmosphere was too weak to scatter the growing sunlight, so even in broad daylight, the stars shone steady. Only Jupiter's omnipresent orb blocked them out. This side of Io always faced the planet, but as it progressed through its day-and-three-quarter orbit, I would see a portion of the giant's colorful bands and eddies close up. Even now, they swirled into view at a stately pace befitting a king, white and brown, yellow and ruddy, astonishingly bright.

I could have immersed myself in this vision until the sun burned out, but then another fire caught my eye, a vast lake of red and orange crusted by cooling rock with a great, dark island squatting in its midst. Beyond, a yellowed ridge belched fire into the sky. This was the tour's final spectacle. The ridge was the volcano Loki and the lake Loki Patera, the hottest spot on Io.

I pressed my face to the window. The IoMobile didn't allow me closer.

Too many people didn't want me to die. Perhaps in my immortality, they found hope for their own. With each funeral I attended, that hope proved vain but fueled my hope that I might find a way to follow them. That may be why I took comfort in the company of the normal elderly, such as Chip Reubens.

Chip's time would come soon enough, but at eighty-three he still had one of the sharpest, most devious minds I had known. In his youth, he'd been a perpetual firebrand, the nemesis of bosses, administrators, and politicians. By now he'd become something of a recluse, but just give him a reason and he'd find a way to upend every table in the temple. Fittingly, he had a wizardly look: bent and frumpy, unruly gray hair, dark eyes that weighed your soul. His reaction to my request was predictable: a bout of cussing that morphed into fascination.

"Waste of money," he fumed. "Waste of time. Toys for the rich, who should be taking care of *this* planet and its people! Buddy of mine hacked into Rimworld and got the specs on those monstrosities. You could drop Mt. Everest on them without scratching the paint." He waved me off and took a gulp from the bottle of chilled water he always kept by his side. The essence of life, he maintained, the secret of his longevity. He planned to make it to one ten, at least, and never let me dissuade him with my doom and gloom speeches. "Anyway, the rescue team would arrive so fast, you'd never miss a breath."

"So how do we do it?" I'd invited him to an outdoor cafe near his old mountainside home, an ancient faux log cabin accessed by dirt road and powered entirely by sun, wind, and geotherm. Chip's self-imposed exile could only be interrupted by an offer of free food. But I'd engaged his brain, now. A warm breeze danced through the table umbrellas as we talked, our sandwiches and chips lying forlorn on their little white plates before us.

"We? What makes you think I want anything to do with it?" He eyed me critically before showing his hand. "We alter their software without tipping them off."

"Can you do that?"

"Yes. Maybe. No." He grinned. "I might know who can."

Which would cost me extra. I picked up my sandwich and took a bite.

"Hell, man, you're loaded. You can afford it."

"I just want to know it'll work."

"Why wouldn't it?" Chip was nothing if not smug. "Half up front, half on successful completion."

Few things got a laugh out of me anymore, but that did. "How do I pay you when I'm dead?"

"Leave it to me in your will. You have a will, don't you?"

I didn't. Why would I?

Easing himself back from the table, Chip smiled at the blue sky. "Get one. You stiff me, I'll find you on the other side."

To its workings, I was clueless. All I know is, four months later Chip delivered a small green stick. Using a holo of the IoMobile's console, he showed me where to plug in the device. Once there, it would do its dirty work by its lonesome. Fifteen seconds later, full control of the vehicle would be mine, and RimWorld wouldn't have a clue.

On the slow-roiling shore of Loki Patera, I plugged it in. I counted the seconds. At fifteen, I put my hands to the controls. I couldn't have picked a better place, surrounded by the universe in all its malevolent beauty. Out of respect for its glory, I offered a moment of silence before taking my leave.

The lake of magma beckoned. The vacuum called my name. The Jovian radiation offered me freedom. And here I sat, listening to them, alone on Io, the eighteenth human to roam its realms of death. In moments I would be the first to perish by its hand. A weighty thought, that, and a distinction for which I was grateful.

I didn't suppose I could savor the moment when it happened, so I played through it now. I could make a sharp turn to the left, and vehicle and I would plunge together into the molten sea. Spectacular, that, but maybe too ostentatious. I could go without fanfare. A quick sequence of commands to open the vehicle's door, and I'd be just as dead.

The red glow flooded the interior of the IoMobile while I weighed my options. There was no sound save the hum of the equipment, yet I fancied I could hear the cauldron's namesake, the trickster Loki, laughing. *All that time*, he mocked, *all that money spent getting here. It's in your grasp, and you sit and gape.*

Sure, I admitted. *It's my last gape. And anyway, don't we all need something to gape at from time to time?*

I remember the thought but not how long it took. At my age, a day passes in the blink of an eye, a year in a breath. Yet it was a spectacular gape. It went on and on while Loki laughed at me and I laughed with him, and in the end, whenever that came, he shook his head and vanished into the sulfur mists, calling over his shoulder, *Call if ever you choose your destiny.*

I suppose I did choose, eventually, but I never called him back. My memory is less than clear. I'm told that when the IoMobile signaled its correct location—because I removed Chip's device at last, although nobody knew but me—I'd exceeded the allotted tour time by nearly eight hours and roamed over twenty kilometers off course. I hadn't blundered into a molten lake, but I'd been near enough to them to frighten everyone at RimWorld from the CEO down to the mechanics who assembled the IoMobile. They debriefed me—interrogated me, to be honest—for days in a vain effort to extract the truth. What could I say? I acted surprised, said I didn't realize anything had gone wrong, swore that I'd had a blast and would love to do it all again. Repeated over and over, that relieved RimWorld's fear of lawsuits if not its perplexity. They'd never had the smallest system failure before, let alone one of this magnitude.

I kept the little green stick to myself and destroyed it at first opportunity. It wouldn't have amused them. I didn't even tell Chip what happened. I didn't need to. He found a reason to come out of isolation at last when I asked him to help me launch a new venture: human exploration of the outer solar system, with myself as the first explorer. A costly, dangerous, time-intensive enterprise, yes, but I could afford both and had no fear of death. I would no longer court it, but if it came, it came.

Ironic how staring death in the face can bring a person back to life. More ironic, still, that a cosmos so hostile to life can be our home. But maybe that's what makes it such a great place to live.

Lesson
(Indies Unlimited Editor's Choice)

Wind whispered in the splintered timbers, murmuring, lamenting. Hearing its agony, Caitlyn nearly cried. "It pines like an abandoned lover."

Mike's expression mocked her though his words fell gentle on her ears. "It's just an old relic. Come on, I'll show you." He tugged her hand.

She refused to budge. "Look at its eyes, Mike."

"Those are windows."

"And the cast of its mouth. It's in pain."

"Don't be silly, Caitlyn. That's a door." His grip tightened. He might have meant to pull her arm off. She dug in her heels, but he was too strong. He'd always been too strong, too determined, too full of himself, oblivious of any feelings but his own.

As they reached the entrance, timbers shifted. Window-eyes and door-mouth widened in alarm. The ruin's pain coursed through her, and something else. Empathy. Anger.

"Mike," she pleaded as he crossed the threshold. She ripped her hand from his and nearly fell.

He turned on her, disdain unmasked. "You're such a baby! I should leave you here. Teach you a lesson."

The decaying rafters groaned. Mike looked up in alarm as the roof collapsed, roaring, all but burying him.

The rest was a blur. She called for help. Police and paramedics extracted Mike from the wreckage. Doctors assured her of his recovery, but she had to honor the house's sacrifice.

So she left him there in the hospital.

Just to teach him a lesson.

Woodsmoke

There's no point telling you why. You wouldn't believe me. Nobody does.

Okay, fine.

I was struck by lightning.

No, not last week. Seven years ago. It changes you, see. It's the finger of God touching you, transforming you. One moment you're ordinary, the next you're dead or permanently scrambled, or sometimes you wake to truths you never suspected. Nobody understands lightning strike survivors, not even doctors. Phantom pains, mood swings, changes in personality, even the inexplicable appearance of new talents, all with no obvious physical cause. Few believe our complaints. Almost nobody believes our gifts.

But they are real. Me, I discovered something profound.

It's hard to explain. Maybe I'd better start at the beginning. Could I have a glass of water? And maybe a chocolate bar?

Thank you.

You know how smells carry memory? For some it's the aroma of home cooking, for others a woman's perfume, for still others the scent of pine or roses. For me, it's woodsmoke. When woodsmoke hangs in the air, I'm transported to my childhood. My dad loved to camp and fish in the mountains. Every summer we'd spend as many weekends as possible up there, plus a whole week for vacation, usually in July. Dad, Mom, my sister Allie, and I would camp by frigid blue lakes, wander up and down rocky slopes, cook over wood fires. Sometimes when the night wasn't too cold, we'd abandon our tents and sleep under the stars.

Have you ever seen the stars up there? The universe folds you in its arms. It's so incredibly alive.

The cooking fires and the evening campfires, though, they were extra special. Woodsmoke bound our experiences into an organic whole. It clung to your clothing and followed you home. When the trip was over, you still smelled the woodsmoke and relived the memories, until mom washed it out. Even after, because whenever we lit a fire in the fireplace, the memories would well up, and I'd be back in the mountains, hiking, fishing, lying beneath the stars.

That was years ago, before the car crash that January. Then suddenly mom and dad were gone. Allie was in college, and I was at the bank taking mortgage applications for people who wanted to bulldoze trees and build houses in their places. We both took it hard, real hard. Allie quit school and never went back. I almost got fired.

Months of misery later, summer returned. We couldn't go on like that, so I suggested we revisit the mountains and remember how it had been. Maybe that would help us lay our parents to rest. So we did, just the two of us. We camped, hiked, cooked over a wood fire, slept under the stars. For most of a week we relived our childhood, until that day a sudden squall caught us hiking on an exposed ridge. I only vaguely remember the world exploding. I woke three days later in the hospital with Allie sobbing at my side. It pained me to see her so sad. I put my hand on her head and stroked her hair to comfort her. Woodsmoke still clung to her.

I first perceived it then, although it was but the embryo of a vision. Allie and I had passed through fire. Literally. We'd been consumed and remade. We'd become different, super-human. To the outside world, we looked the same. I still processed loans at the bank and got Allie a job as a teller. We bought a cheap two-bedroom house together, an abused foreclosure with a fenced backyard and a fireplace in the living room.

We worked on fixing it up, and every night we built a fire and sat by it, watching the flames dance, inhaling stray wisps of woodsmoke.

The smoke whispered to us. It taught us things, things most people don't know, things you, Detective Havel, never dreamed. Like most people, you think you're important, your possessions are important, your likes and dislikes and even your whims are important. But you, your wife, your children, your grandchildren, you are all just smoke wafting on the wind. That's all you are, all any of us are. The whole cosmos is smoke. It's an illusion. You can't fight it, Detective. You *mustn't* fight it. The only peace lies in embracing this wisdom.

I can tell you don't believe me. Nobody does. It's not really your fault. It's a hard truth to see and even harder to accept. Even Allie didn't see it at first. I think that's because I took the brunt of the lightning. It only tickled her skin. But she, at least, was open to learning. I taught her by the fireplace, or rather, the woodsmoke taught her. She gradually awakened, but chimneys siphon off most of the smoke. In time, she needed more than a fireplace could offer. We found a spot away from everything where we could build campfires, then bonfires. We built them larger and larger as our minds expanded, and eventually we walked together into, shall we say, Nirvana.

It explains *everything*, Detective Havel. You're just not listening.

Yes, I taught her and prepared her, but she took the final step herself, and what a brilliant step it was. She burned a whole forest! Through that forest fire, she consummated our vision.

You still don't see, do you? Listen, Detective. Listen! With enough woodsmoke, we can enlighten the whole world!

Dust

(Indies Unlimited Editor's Choice Honorable Mention)

Dry clouds billowed over the land, kicked up by the combines trundling through the parched wheat. Blown by a hot July wind, the dust masqueraded as warm fog bearing moisture to break the drought.

Mockery, Julian thought. He watched atop a rise above the expanse of his Uncle Brandon's fields. The harvest had proven more chaff than grain, giving the lie to their supplier's claims. These new seeds had been engineered—so the brochures said—to thrive in the drying climate. Instead, they were driving Brandon to bankruptcy.

In his left hand, Julian's cell phone vibrated. He glanced at the incoming call. Maggie, his girlfriend, looking for him. She mustn't know he was here. He had no business in the field. Nobody did. Brandon had invested in automated combines five years ago, when farming still looked viable. Now the machines were more liability than asset. Julian knew, because he helped with the books. The farm wouldn't survive another year.

Maggie's call went to voice mail. She wouldn't like it, but he'd explain later how, distraught, he had wandered the banks of the dry stream a mile south of here, worrying about the future. She'd understand. The dust clouded her family's fortunes, too. It clouded everyone's. But not for long.

He punched a number into his phone. Fire blossomed in the belly of one of the combines, devoured the dry grass, and engulfed the other machines. It roared over the fields, unstoppable, no respecter of property lines.

He tucked his phone into his pocket and turned away. Once the shock subsided, Uncle Brandon could call his insurance company. Everyone could. And Julian?

He was just happy to help.

The Bamboo Carrier

The cubicle farm.

That's how Timur Kalashnik characterized the rows of desks and walls and cabinetry filling the cavernous fourth floor office where he worked. Dark steel jutted like rocks from the pseudo-soil of the rich brown carpet, while flower gardens of pushpins blossomed on tan fabric partitions, a modernist portrayal in which nature had been bent, stretched, and superimposed upon the artificial.

But the mop of greenery processing down the next row over from his desk, *that* was real. It was mid-Monday morning when Timur watched it bob over the partitions, moving left to right from one end of the office to the other, slow, deliberate, rustling in the breeze of its own passage. Then it shook itself and started the return trip, arriving a few minutes later right back where it started.

That wasn't the end of its walk. It turned and began another circuit, then another, back and forth, back and forth, four times in all, before ducking into the cubicle where its journey began.

Odd behavior for a plant, Timur thought, or even for someone carrying a plant, but it didn't surprise him much. He'd known plenty of odd folk in his life. Like his father. Timur had grown up on a Minnesota farm, the son of a Russian refugee who slipped through the folds in the Iron Curtain a mere four years before it rent for good. Father liked Minnesota as much as he liked anywhere. "Just like Siberia," he used to tell Timur, "but with bread in the store." People thought him peculiar. He was always looking over his shoulder, always apologizing for other people's mistakes, always dreading shadows in the night. Timur could never have friends over late. Darkness made Father edgy. He would neither venture into it nor let others face it if he could stop them. Heavy curtains shut out the dark each evening, and a hush overtook their home. No TV, no radio. Even book pages had to be turned silently.

Timur asked Mother about it one summer day while Father was out in the fields. He was only nine, tall for his age, lanky, and curious about everything. A friend from school had received a telescope for his birthday and invited Timur to look through it some night, but Father refused permission. Why? What was so sinister about the stars?

Mother smiled and stroked his golden hair, hair the color of her own. Her people had come from Sweden in the long ago, not Russia, but she seemed to understand Father when no one else did. "Nothing at all," she said. "But your father has bad memories."

"About the stars?" he asked.

"About many things. About the night."

Timur never found out more. Father wouldn't speak of his fears, nor would Mother. He felt a bit like that plant, wandering up and down the aisle, back and forth, over and over, getting nowhere.

But today, work beckoned. He was a number cruncher now, a man who analyzed and synthesized and reported to more powerful men who rendered money-making decisions that filled other people's bank accounts. It was a living. It even allowed him to buy his own telescope. He never convinced Father to join him under the stars, but sometimes in the daylight they wandered the moon's rugged surface together or swooped low over the fires of the sun. Stars didn't bother Father when he saw them in the bright light of day.

About noon, the plant got up for another walk. Its shaggy crown danced above the cubicle walls, back and forth, back and forth. Timur spotted it halfway through its first crossing and couldn't take his eyes from it. It made four round-trips, as before, then settled back at its desk, out of sight.

He shook his head and resumed tapping on his keyboard.

At three o'clock, it rose and embarked upon a third progress through the office realm. This time, Timur timed it. Four round trips, two and a half minutes each, ten minutes start to finish. He opened a new spreadsheet and recorded start time, end time, and total duration.

On Tuesday, the plant repeated its performance, and on Wednesday, too. He logged each excursion, three every day, at ten o'clock, noon, and three, four round trips each time, ten minutes per cycle. Convinced the plant was going on walkabout to a schedule, he set reminders in his calendar so he wouldn't miss them. He hopped on the internet to research plants and found the green mop consisted of bamboo leaves. He investigated motives, too, but found nothing on taking bamboo for a walk, neither as horticultural practice nor mystical experience. The conundrum began to gnaw at his brain.

By three o'clock Friday as the greenery jiggled above the cubicle walls, Timur realized this couldn't go on. That damn plant was eating up all his time, what with observing, recording, charting, researching, and pondering. His personal productivity dropped to zero every time it swished by and didn't lift much above it in the interregna. *Somebody* must be carrying it for *some* purpose, and he wouldn't divine who or why by watching its leaves dance. On Monday, he resolved, he would confront the bamboo carrier.

He spent most of Saturday and Sunday planning the showdown. Only later did he wonder why he'd wasted a perfectly good weekend on *that*.

Monday morning, nine fifty-five. Timur rose from his desk and made for the end of the office, where he rounded the corner and planted himself like a rock at the turning point in the bamboo's path. A moment later, its green top rose above the wall of the cubicle at the far end of the row, and out of the cubicle stepped…

…someone, anyway. He thought it was a woman, but between the distance and the way the (alleged) she held the plant in front of her (supposed) face, it was impossible to be sure. Whoever it was wore a faded pair of jeans and seemed on the short side. Yet the apparition had bearing. Person and plant approached with such dignity, such solemnity, that Timur felt an urge to kneel.

The minutes passed, five in all, before the bamboo carrier arrived before him. By then her identity—it was indeed a woman—stood revealed. A mere five foot two with gray hair pulled back in a pony tail and a face full of wrinkles, she smiled at him, her eyes a gentle brown, her hands encircling the white ceramic pot as though in prayer. She wore a green blouse about the color of the bamboo leaves and a pair of white sneakers that whispered along the carpet.

She turned and began her return journey before Timur could speak. He didn't know what he'd expected, but she wasn't it. Gathering his scattered wits, he hurried to catch up and walked beside her in silence until they reached her desk, whereupon they turned as one and began the second circuit.

"Most people ignore me," she said. She grinned at the bamboo.

"Well," Timur replied.

"Well," she agreed.

"I sit over there." He waved in the generally correct direction. "I saw the leaves."

"Nice, aren't they? Pandas eat them, you know."

"Do you have a panda?" Now why had he asked *that*?

She shook her head without suggesting the question was unreasonable.

Timur, though, found nothing at all reasonable here. "So why…" He waved vaguely at the bamboo.

"My doctor says I should walk thirty minutes a day," the woman replied. "By the way, my name is Alice."

"I'm Timur."

"What kind of name is that?"

"Russian."

Alice's face scrunched up, just for an instant. "If I walk for thirty minutes, my legs fall off. So I walk for ten minutes, instead, three times a day."

The figure matched Timur's spreadsheet, anyway. "Do you get the same benefit?" he asked.

"Who cares? I can tell the good doctor I do my thirty minutes." She flashed him a sly grin.

"What about the bamboo? What's that for?"

"Extra credit. It builds upper body strength. It's kind of heavy. See?" Without stopping, she thrust the plant at him.

He took it from her and weighed it in his hands. It didn't seem heavy to him, but then she *was* a little old lady. He passed it back. "So this is all about exercise?"

Alice laughed. "Or making you ask questions."

They finished the second back-and-forth in silence and moved on to the third. Timur had been so sure some wonderful curiosity awaited discovery beneath the bamboo leaves that the reality proved a massive let-down. He should have returned to work, but somehow he thought she might need his company. Or *vice versa*. She didn't object but held her silence for another half circuit. Then she said, "You don't have an accent."

"My father came from Russia. I was born here."

"My little brother married a woman from Russia." She turned the pot in her hands and brushed quickly at the leaves as though removing cobwebs. "What does your father say about Russia?"

"Nothing," Timur said. "Nothing at all."

Alice handed him the bamboo again. "You carry it for a while. I'm developing too much upper body strength."

He couldn't help but chuckle as he received the plant.

Brushing off her hands, Alice said, "My sister-in-law was married before, in the old country."

"What happened to her husband?"

She shrugged.

Timur wondered if she didn't know or if, like his parents, she only wished she didn't know. He could wish he wasn't curious about such things, things that caused others so much pain, but he couldn't help it. He wanted to know why his father feared the night. He wanted them both to venture out under the stars. Because even in the darkness, there was beauty and light.

"Better let me have that back now," Alice said as they made the turn for the final crossing. She took the bamboo and cradled it against her chest. "He's my green baby. He almost died the month after I bought him."

"He looks fine now." Timur nearly slapped himself for calling a plant "he."

"Yes," she agreed. "He doesn't believe in letting past trauma define his future." She made like she was bench pressing the bamboo, then she grinned at Timur. "If you want some exercise, you can join me anytime. We can get another bamboo plant, and I'll be your personal trainer."

Timur thought he might take her up on that, at least from time to time.

For Emergency Use Only

It just figured, didn't it?

Lights dead, refrigerator dead, TV dead, *everything* dead, and now cellular service dispersed like a puff of cigarette smoke on the January wind. Tyler speculated that if he smoked, the cigarettes would have run out, too, as Karen had run out, leaving him to face the power outage alone. She could have canceled her trip when the forecast turned dire, but no, money beckoned, so she swapped tickets for an earlier flight instead. She had already descended through the New York clouds and was probably sipping wine with other agents or publishers by the time the storm stretched forth its icy fingers and throttled Madison, Wisconsin.

So here lies Tyler, flopped on the couch, unable to commute to his own job, useless cell phone in hand, feeling the temperature sink quarter degree by quarter degree. He looked out the window at the ice-caked world, at branches sagging and cracking inside crystalline sheaths, and thought, *Why the WiFi?*

If he had a signal, he could answer that. The almighty Web would know if ice could scramble microwaves or pull down cell towers. But he couldn't pray to that god for answers now. It had turned its back on him, refusing him even the answer given Job: *Where were* you *when my electrons began to flow?*

Tyler glared at the phone's useless screen. In response, it slipped into battery saver mode.

Fine, he decided. *I'll make up my own answer.* He imagined a foot-thick crust of blue-white ice warping a steel giant until it buckled at the knees and crashed to the ground, raising a spray of white powder, its death rattle echoing through the hills. A satisfying image, that. He replayed the mental video and morphed it into an epic battle between an ice giant and a mechanized behemoth, stomping forests, fields, and villages into the frozen earth as they crashed upon each other again and again. The battle raged clear across the state, west to Minnesota, south to Illinois, east to Lake Michigan, until the monsters dragged each other into the frigid waters and drowned.

Now *that* was a movie!

Tyler picked up the TV remote, pushed the power button, and stared at the blank forty-eight inch flat-screen mounted on the wall. He tapped the buttons to scroll through the channel guide, every line of which was the same empty black. *Football game*, he thought. *There ought to be a football game later today.* But the only game he'd see today, apparently, was in his mind. He rose from the couch, remote gripped in his right hand, and searched the far side of the room for his wide receiver. He dodged left, skittered right, twisted, aimed, fired! The remote sailed across the room into the waiting arms of the recliner, which caught it with a dull thud.

First down!

From deep in his opponent's territory, he manufactured a spectacular drive, crossing the fifty, the forty, closer and closer to the goal line. But alas, a sack and a near-fumble later, he lost steam. It was third and eight in easy field goal range, but he wasn't about to place kick the remote. It was a bad day for a broken window. So time ran out. He never determined the score but claimed victory anyway.

So much for the big game. What time was it by now? Tyler picked up his cell phone to check, but it had passed from battery saver mode to dead. He dropped it on the couch and shoved his hands in his pockets. He could have bought a watch. He could have bought a battery-powered wall clock. But no. Cell phones had clocks, so why bother? His only actual clock was the plug-in on his nightstand. He didn't even know if it was time to be hungry. Worse, he couldn't call Karen or any-one else to find out if it was time to be hungry.

Hell with it. He made a peanut butter sandwich anyway and risked opening the refrigerator long enough to pour a glass of milk. Then he did it again to locate the strawberry preserves, because pea-nut butter was twice as good with strawberries. The refrigerator wasn't much of a problem anyway. If the food started to warm up, he could stuff it into the snow.

Tyler took his plate and glass back to the couch, retrieved the remote, and surfed around until he found the original *Star Wars* film on one of the movie channels. Okay, the entry was black, but he could see it vividly enough in his mind's eye. He pushed play and ran through as much of the dialogue as he could remember while eating. The food ran out before the script, but that was fine. He didn't want to get up and do the dishes anyway. For one thing, the dishwasher wasn't about to start. He really should have run it last night. Oh, well.

What, Tyler wondered, *did people do before electricity and cell phones and the Internet and DVRs? How could anyone possibly live like this for more than twenty minutes?*

To keep from going crazy, he imagined the well-appointed Nean-derthal cave, complete with all the wireless devices one could build with stone: granite televisions with quartz screens, sandstone cell phones in decorative feldspar cases, oyster shell headphones. (He couldn't figure out earbuds. Anything a Neanderthal might have shoved in his ear would likely cause pain.) By the time he was done building his Stone Age dream home, he almost wanted to live there, except he had no interest in hunting mastodons. Tyler enjoyed a good steak as much as the next person, but he'd rather someone else did the butchering.

So he returned himself to the present and the dishes to the kitchen sink. The water, at least, still ran. With luck it wouldn't freeze before the heat came back on. Speaking of which, a distinct chill had infiltrated the homestead. He mounted the dim stairs and went into the bedroom to retrieve a sweater from the dresser. As he pulled it on, he pondered taking a nap. That could make the day bearable, particularly if the power came on while he slept.

He sat on his side of the bed and looked at the clock, the plug-in clock that even when not running would at least be right twice a day. A thick book rested beside it. On the cover—a garish rendering of a space battle—a yellow sticky note had been stuck. He peeled off the note and read what Karen had penned.

For emergency use only.

Tyler propped up the pillows, settled into them, and opened the book. The snowy light streaming through the window lit up the page. He didn't know the title or author, but he might as well see if it was a tenth as good as *Star Wars.* A page or three ought to suffice.

When the power came on three and a half hours later, Tyler was too engrossed in the story to notice.

Angry Bird
(Indies Unlimited Editor's Choice)

"I don't like the look on that bird's face," Frank said through the side of his mouth.

"Who's looking at her face?" Will replied with a smirk.

"Not the woman! The *bird*!" Frank pointed. They were standing in the wet sand along the shore, waves lapping at their bare feet. Farther along, a pretty young lady in a pretty skimpy swimsuit was washing a shell in the water. The little white bird, though, only half as far away, had murder in his eyes.

"Who cares about birds?" Will said. "I'm gonna meet her." He marched off toward his romantic destiny, leaving Frank to stare after him.

The bird turned as Will passed it by and screeched like a set of worn out tires.

"Shut up," Will snapped, flapping his arm at it. "Fly south for the summer."

The bird took wing, not south but straight for Will. Frank watched in horror as the creature's beak opened to dozens of times its body size and swallowed Will whole. Then he did the only rational thing he could. He passed out.

The woman sauntered up to the bird and patted it on the head. "Good boy," she said. "Shall we go home?"

Adoption

It didn't seem so awful, running beneath the crystalline skies in the calm after the storm. He was disobeying Mom, but he'd done it so often, and always Dad laughed it off, which deflected her anger. But this night, he was wrong.

As the storm retreated north in the falling dark, the all-clear sounded. Len Vandermeullen was out the door like a snake striking. He scampered through sodden gardens kicking up mud, down the tree-dotted hill from the Secretary's Mansion to the open field inside the compound fence. He skidded to a halt, turned his eyes heavenward, and pressed his new astrospecs to his face. His father had given him the device last month for his fourteenth birthday. He practiced with them every clear night.

The stars had called Len since before he could read. He was quite the astronomer, so his science teachers said. He knew every constellation and bright star. Rising in the east, the Spacecraft swooped past Armstrong the Explorer; near the zenith, the Bearshark's gaping jaws roared; southward, the Silverbow Tree spread its branches from the horizon, its crown glittering with white, blue, orange, and red stars. With his astrospecs, he sought out the unknown, stars too dim to have names, clusters that looked like tiny clouds, dark holes seemingly punched in the universe by obscuring nebulae. Using eye movements and winks, he highlighted whatever caught his fancy, and the astropecs served up delicious information: magnitudes, distances, ages, masses, sizes. He feasted on it all.

And that was the danger Mom feared. Gorging himself on the cosmos, he missed what was closer to home. The storm, now far north, ablaze with lightning, sending thunder rumbling through the hills, might be followed by another, and another. "There's a reason," she warned time and again, "why the world is called Rudra." She had never explained, neither the name nor the reason, but Len knew storms. Weather fascinated him, too. Rudra's primary star and its distant secondary created complex patterns of differential heating, while the planet's rapid rotation stirred the pot. Furious storms could ignite and swell in less than an hour. Sometimes they came in pairs, triplets even. When the warning klaxons sounded, you had but minutes to take shelter. The all-clear only meant the known danger had passed. The unknown could spring upon you minutes later.

But Len didn't much care. Though Mom fretted, Dad relished and encouraged his enthusiasm for science, and Dad was the Planetary Secretary, second in power to the Governor. Mom *had* to listen to Dad, hadn't she? Besides, Len could run. He'd timed the dash up the hill to the house and knew he could make it, should the warning ring out, before the first lightning seared the sky, before the first hurricane gust punched his face.

Basically, Len thought, *I'm invincible.* And so he prowled the skies without fear, searching out awe.

Suddenly it was there near the zenith, a bright star he'd never seen before. The astrospecs didn't know it, either, which made no sense. They could only tell him its brightness: magnitude two point three.

How could an object that bright not be in the database?

The device changed its mind. Magnitude two point two.

Two point one.

Two point zero.

It was brightening! Len whipped off the astrospecs and squinted, breath held, body rock steady. He compared the new star to familiar ones nearby. And yes, very slowly, almost imperceptibly, its light grew.

A minute passed, maybe two, maybe five, maybe five thousand. Why would a star brighten like that? Was it a supernova? Had he actually discovered such a rare phenomenon in the moment it happened? The star now blazed brighter than any other, and then the impossible happened. It didn't just brighten, it grew, expanding from scintillating point to fat oval to irregular and boxy. Something was falling from space, not with a fireball flash that blazed and was gone, but controlled, deliberate.

A spacecraft!

Warning klaxons screamed. Len barely heard them, but he knew today he wouldn't make the top of the hill. Whatever was happening, he couldn't escape. What did this mean, a spacecraft landing in the middle of the city, in the planetary government compound, almost atop the Governor's Mansion?

I'm sorry, Mom, he heard himself whisper. *I'm sorry!*

A barrage of lighting erupted, not storm lightning but weapons fire from the descending ship, and the world became a blaze of red engulfed in heat and smoke. Len dropped the astrospecs and ran. His legs ached as he powered up the hill through burning trees and slippery mud, running for the house, running for his life, running for his mother who appeared in the doorway, panic etched on her face, her arms stretched out as though she might touch him in spite of the distance.

Before he could get there, the ground heaved and the sky roared and the night swallowed him whole.

A hissing, a squealing, like steam escaping an antique kettle. The choking smell of burned synthetics and molten metal. Len gagged. Something sharp gouged his left ribs. He rolled away to escape the skewer, but the pain followed. Voices in the distance cried and screamed and shouted. He couldn't open his eyes for fear of what he might see.

Something crunched nearby, something heavy marching through rubble. Whatever it was stopped near his head. He kept still, knowing it wasn't a friend. He barely breathed, sensing he was being scrutinized by cold eyes and colder minds. He squeezed his eyes tight, hoping the invaders would leave. Then a hand touched his face and brushed something from his skin.

"Take him to Cranmore." A woman's clear alto, strong, no-nonsense, both like and unlike Mom's.

"Just kill him," a ragged male voice said. "He's half dead anyway."

Len felt tears squeeze from his closed eyes. They stung. He couldn't even blink them away for fear of moving. He heard the crack of a hand striking a face, then he was lifted roughly, and pain engulfed him. He nearly threw up but passed out instead.

"Took you long enough."

The voice was different, quiet, withered, like somebody's great-grandfather standing graveside moments before toppling in. The light was bright now, or brighter anyway, enough to make Len squint.

"Kids are supposed to be fast healers."

Len blinked at the face that accompanied the voice. The man wasn't half as old as he sounded. His thinning hair was in disarray, his face scarred and creased, as though he had spent his whole life worrying over problems he couldn't solve. He was dressed in a threadbare gray coverall.

"Where..." Len's throat was dry.

"Oh," the man said. "The eternal questions. Figures."

Len coughed. He hadn't the strength to cover his mouth.

The man elaborated: "Where the hell am I, how the hell did I get here, and where the hell am I going?"

Len licked his lips. They were dry and cracked.

"Hospital. More or less." The man lifted Len's arm and checked his pulse. "Less than more, but you make do with what you have." He dropped Len's wrist.

Len guessed the city hospital was destroyed. This must be an emergency hospital. "What happened?"

"Now *that* is a very big question. The universe is thirteen billion years old and full of stuff happening every nanosecond, while most of us are very small." The man chuckled at his own humor.

"I mean…" Len licked his lips again. He wished for water but wasn't sure it was safe to ask.

"I know what you mean." The man helped Len sit and passed him a translucent bottle with a tube protruding from the top. "Sip slow."

Len sipped. The liquid had a strange, soapy taste. He made a face.

"My favorite, too. I'm Cranmore. Doctor Cranmore, but we're neither formal nor proud here. Doctor is just one more job, and hardly a glamorous one." Cranmore put a hand on Len's shoulder, maybe to comfort him, maybe to test something, then helped Len lie back down. "So, you want to know what happened. You don't, really, but I'll tell you anyway. Your city was attacked and looted. A lot of people died. I'm sorry."

Len swallowed. *What about Mom? What about Dad?* He could barely think it, much less speak it.

"Be glad you met with fortune, boy. You could have died, too. Instead, you were rescued by one of the very few big people in the universe." Cranmore looked entirely serious as he folded his arms over his chest and stepped away. In his place, a woman came to Len's bedside.

His breath caught in his throat when he saw her. Her dark eyes pierced him. Her light brown hair, hanging in ringlets, framed a lean face, a face of authority, of command. She wasn't as tall as the doctor, yet in presence she was ten times his size.

"Name," she said. A demand, not a question.

He tried to push himself up, but his head swam. He flopped back.

"I didn't say get up. I said, name."

He didn't want to answer. He couldn't not. "Len."

"Leonard?"

"Just Len."

The woman drew near, grasped his chin, turned his head to look him square in the eyes. To his astonishment, she smiled, if slightly. "Len. Lenny. Welcome aboard." She released him. Still commanding his eyes, she asked Cranmore, "Prognosis?"

"He's fine. Skewered below the right rib cage, but reasonably shallow. No infection. Otherwise, just minor injuries. He should be fit for duty in two or three days."

The woman nodded.

Len didn't understand. "I want to go home. I want my parents."

"I'm your mother now," the woman said.

Panic engulfed him. Fighting dizziness, he sat. "No, you're not! I want to go *home*!"

The woman perched on the edge of the bed and ran a hand through his hair. Her touch wasn't harsh, but he didn't like it. He wanted her to leave.

"I know it's hard. Your home is gone, your parents dead. You're my son now. This is your home now. You're one of us." She stood.

"I don't even know who you are!" Len objected, as though that would make her vanish, bring his parents running, transport him home.

The woman's eyes swallowed him, swallowed the whole of the cosmos. One of the few big people of the universe Cranmore had called her. As Len looked into her eyes, he could believe there was none bigger.

"Everyone knows me," she said. "I'm Anna Grande." She waited just long enough to see recognition blossom in his shocked face, then she was gone.

Fear overtook Len. "Oh, no."

Cranmore cocked his head. "Oh, no? God, Len, how many boys d'you think get to call Anna Grande mother? It's an honor, one hell of an honor."

"She's a pirate. A murderer!"

The doctor drew near. "Sure," he whispered. "And she's just like you." He tousled Len's hair and smiled mischievously. "Why do you think she saved you?"

The days passed in a blur. In his waking hours, Len longed for home and his parents and wished the nightmare would end. Sleeping, more nightmares invaded, half-remembered chases through fire and destruction from which he awoke in a cold sweat. But his strength returned quickly, and before long Cranmore pronounced him fit for duty, whereupon he discovered it wasn't an expression.

He was assigned a succession of jobs, mostly cleaning and minor repair work. He hated it. The jobs were dull and repetitive and in the service of the woman who had killed his parents. Rage and guilt filled him each time he recalled her ship, this ship, the *Liberator*, descend upon them. He should have realized, should have raised the alarm, should have saved everyone. Not that he could have, but his impotence made it worse.

Worst of all, he wasn't immune to the romanticism of Anna Grande, the unpredictable, the uncatchable, arch-nemesis of the Earth Security force, bane of the outer territories. Every boy filled with adventure lust followed or fought her, every girl wanted to be her as she plundered through space, preying on cargo ships, transports, even military vessels, stealing and kidnapping at will. That had been the way of it throughout colonized space for twenty-four years Earth standard. But to meet her face to face, to be forced to join her crew…

He only escaped guilt and anger when helping Cranmore, who Len couldn't help but call Doctor despite the old man's protestations. Len couldn't see Cranmore as a pirate, not when he was so wise and kind, not surrounded by the trappings of medicine and science, primitive as they were.

Cranmore taught him everything, including how to access information from the ship's data stores, which proved as rich a library as any Len had ever known. Before long, the doctor even inducted him into the practice of medicine. A young woman came to the hospital with a nasty cut high on her left thigh received during battle training. Cranmore instructed Len in cleaning and sealing the wound. The woman was amused by Len's embarrassment and awkwardness, even when his clumsiness caused her pain. But in the end, Cranmore praised his work.

After their patient left, Len asked, "Where is she from?"

"Tria? She works in the galley most of the time."

"I mean before she was here."

Cranmore busied himself with sterilizing the equipment and motioned Len to clean the surgical table. "That's complicated."

Len started scrubbing the surface. "I guess I have time."

"Short version, her parents were part of the original crew. They brought her along for the ride."

"On a pirate ship?"

"What were they supposed to do? They couldn't leave her. She was only seven."

That seemed wrong. Tria hardly looked thirty-one.

Cranmore gave him a disappointed teacher look. "Yes, Anna Grande has been on the loose for twenty-four years, but she gets around. Remember your Special Relativity, Len. Ship's time, she's only been plundering for fifteen years. Biologically, Tria is twenty-two."

Len finished wiping down the table and tossed the cleaning cloth into the incinerator. A buzz signaled the reduction of the material to its constituent components. "Why did her parents join the crew?"

"I already told you." Cleanup done, Cranmore motioned Len out of the procedure room to reception, where an older woman was busy working a computer display embedded in a countertop. "Watch this," he told Len quietly. He addressed the woman. "Len wants to know why you came aboard, Falak."

She turned. She had light brown skin, wrinkled and severe, but her voice was soft. "That's complicated," she said. She smiled curtly and turned back to her work.

"There you go," Cranmore said. "Every story here is complicated, and often too painful to voice. Just like yours. Why did you come aboard, Len?"

Len looked at his shoes and shrugged.

"Complicated," Cranmore agreed. "Family always is."

"You're not my family!" Len snapped. He turned away, embarrassed at having yelled at Cranmore. He ought to apologize, but he couldn't. He wouldn't. His family was dead, and Cranmore pledged his allegiance to their murderer. The doctor might as well have killed them with his scalpel.

Cranmore busied himself with a report on the computer display.

"Some of us," Falak said, still engaged in her work, voice still soft, "joined in desperation. Some in anger. Some were conscripted. Some were born here. None are blood relatives of Anna Grande, but we are her family. She has no other. Nor do we, any longer. She's our matriarch, and we're all loyal to her."

Len remembered Anna Grande's voice as she declared herself his mother. It wasn't harsh or cruel, but she had given him no choice. "Why?" he asked.

Falak turned, eyes wide with astonishment. "Why? Because she's given us everything. It's right and proper to be grateful." She turned back to her work and added, "Besides, the alternative is death."

Over his first two months aboard *Liberator*, Len worked every part of the ship, cleaning, repairing, operating, upgrading. His head crammed full of schematics and procedures, he could almost operate the vessel himself. Almost. He may be a quick study, but there was so much to learn, and each day he discovered something new. Boring tasks gave way to more interesting ones: propulsion, environment, computer operations. He felt a growing fascination for the ship, but beneath that festered resentment, keeping him apart from the crew. They helped him and encouraged him to become one of them, but he couldn't permit them too near, not when they gave allegiance to his parents' killer.

He was assisting the quartermaster, a thin, ragged man named Harlan Connor, review inventory records when Anna Grande arrived and with a glance dismissed all but Len from her presence. Seated at a computer desk, he rose. She motioned him down and circled behind him, scrutinizing him. He waited, barely breathing. If he'd had a weapon, he might have killed her, or tried to. Everyone knew you couldn't kill Anna Grande.

"Made yourself at home?" she asked.

Len didn't answer. This would never be his home.

"Don't pine, Lenny. You can't restore what's gone. This moment, right here, right now, is all you ever have."

"Is that why you kill and steal? To get what you can right now?" The rebuke spilled out before he could catch it. He didn't care. Let her kill him. Death would be better than living under her rule.

Anna Grande neither answered nor struck him down. She rounded the desk, stopped opposite him, and studied his eyes, a predator sizing up her prey. He couldn't look away. He resented her power over him even as he succumbed to it.

"I don't explain myself to anyone, Lenny. Not even you."

"Because you're the Captain?"

"Because I'm Anna Grande. Remember that."

"I can't forget it." Len wished he could spit the words in her face. "I can't ever forget what you did. *Captain.*"

Her face remained as impassive as stone. "The others call me Captain. Not you."

"What do I call you?"

"What did you call your mother?"

He lowered his eyes so she wouldn't see the hurt, but he couldn't keep it from his voice. "Mom."

"That's what you call me."

He slammed his fist on the desk and sprang to his feet, shaking with rage. "You *killed* my mother!"

Strangely, sympathy crept into Anna Grande's smoky eyes. "No, Lenny. Not me."

"I was there. I saw."

"Rudra's planetary governor, a swindler named Harlow Cornwall, killed your parents."

That couldn't be. He knew Harlow Cornwall. The governor had been his parents' friend. He'd always had a kind word for Len and sometimes gifts.

"Sit down," Anna Grande told him, her voice unusually gentle. Len sat. "I kill and steal when I must, but it's far easier to bargain. I had an agreement with Cornwall. He went back on his word. The fool should have known better." She arched her eyebrows in query.

Len swallowed. Everyone knew you didn't double-cross Anna Grande.

"Had Cornwall been honest, your parents would be alive. A lot of people would be. And you'd still be on Rudra, gazing up at the stars."

"How did you know—"

"Cranmore mentioned your interests. You must have told him. Unless he's psychic."

He didn't remember telling Cranmore, but the doctor certainly knew Len's interests.

"Now you're sailing the stars," Anna Grande added. "I'd say you've traded up. So…" She stretched out her hand, and for the first time Len noticed she was holding something. It looked like his lost astrospecs but more sleek, more elegant, with lenses that could be raised and lowered. He took the device and examined it.

"Infospecs," she explained. "Keyed to *Liberator's* network. I've given you read access to everything. Behave yourself, and someday I may give you control."

"Everything?" He'd heard about this tech. Infospecs were used to operate industrial processes, transports, military vessels. With them, you could manage solar power collection, navigate spacecraft, plan and execute battles. With access to her entire network, Len might gather enough information to destroy her. Why would she give him such power?

"How old are you, Lenny? Fifteen?"

"Fourteen."

"Why do you think I'm here?"

He could only repeat what he'd heard. "I guess that's complicated."

Humor brightened her eyes, and she laughed like a girl, but the transformation unwound as quickly as it had come. "You know how old I was when I got my first ship?"

Len didn't. The stories didn't say. Anna Grande was a titan sprung full-formed from the ether. She could be a billion years old for all he knew.

"Eighteen," she said, "and scared stiff. I didn't ask for a ship. It was there when I needed it. So I took it, and I've been Anna Grande ever since."

"Weren't you always?"

"I was a different Anna Grande then. Tragedy changes us, sometimes for the better, sometimes for the worse. It will change you, Lenny, whether you like it or not."

He put on the infospecs. The display came to life, edging the view of his surroundings with dozens of symbols he didn't understand.

"You'll be working with the navigation team for the next few months. Once you've mastered it, I'll put you on weaponry."

Suddenly light-headed, he flipped up the lenses. "You want me to fight?" He remembered treating the wound on Tria's leg.

"You'll get hand-to-hand training eventually, but this is special, Lenny. Not everyone learns ship's weaponry."

Anger resurfaced. "I'm not a pirate. I'm not fighting for you."

Anna Grande faced him, unruffled but no longer with sympathy. She stood, a barrier between past and present, refusing him access to what he'd lost, offering him a future he was sure to loath. When she spoke, her voice was matter-of-fact.

"You'll do as I say."

He looked away, jaw locked, eyes ablaze.

"Right?"

He wanted to say no, but he had grown weary and wanted her gone. "Yes," he muttered.

"Yes what?"

What might she do to force him to say it? He almost didn't care. But he said it nonetheless, just to be rid of her. "Yes, Mom."

When he finally looked back, he was alone.

Navigation proved harder than any subject Len had ever studied. On Rudra, navigation systems were built into everything and did all the work. "Space ain't like that," Kayla Stetson told him his first day on the job. "You got lots of unknowns out there, lots of gravity bumps and ruts to throw you off course."

She was nineteen, lean, strong, intense, with hair like the summer sun. Len found sitting beside her unsettling. All he could think of was her. She knew it, too, and smirked whenever his thoughts strayed too far from work. But she never said a word, neither to encourage nor discourage his attention, and gradually he learned the subject.

"It's an art," Kayla explained as they worked out the course to their next destination, a tiny mining colony on the edge of some remote solar system Len had never heard of, a place called Yellowknife. "It's what you know plus what you guess plus what you feel. You got the computer, but that's just a start. You gotta second guess it, and the universe."

Len watched her porcelain fingers work the desktop display. He only half understood her actions and knew she expected questions, but he couldn't think of any. He could only watch her delicate movements.

She nudged the computer's recommended line to create a new path. "Know why I did that?" she asked.

"Uh."

She smirked again. "A recent slow collision between two minor planets created a contact binary. The gravity well's here now. The charts don't show it yet. How'd I know?"

"Uh."

"Talked to the port on Yellowknife. Navigation's contacts as well as computers. Who you know plus what you know."

Len wanted to impress Kayla with an insightful question, but only one came to mind, and it was nothing to do with navigation. "Why are we going there?"

"Supplies. Hydrogen for the engines, mostly. They extract it from the ice. Captain has a deal with them. We get it cheap."

In exchange for their lives, probably. Anna Grande said deals were easier than killing, but threats must make negotiations shorter.

Kayla gave him a funny look. Had she guessed his thoughts? If so, she didn't let on. "We monitor and correct our flight path en route. You got a lot of variables to track. Unknown objects, unexpected variations in the interstellar medium, variable engine output..."

She went on and on, but Len's mind was no longer on the lesson or his teacher. He was thinking of revenge.

When his shift ended, Len sequestered himself in his bunk with his infospecs. Privacy didn't exist on *Liberator*. Only Anna Grande had private quarters. Her officers were quartered together apart from the crew, who were assigned bunks in two large, cramped compartments. Families bunked together, but otherwise men, women and children were intermixed in each compartment. He quickly learned you didn't pay attention to what others were doing, but Len couldn't shake the embarrassed feeling that everyone watched him undressing, dressing, and sleeping.

At least with the infospecs on, he could pretend the place was deserted. Hidden behind them, he studied the communications systems and learned their operation. Intraship calls proved easy and largely unsecured, but intership communication required security clearance. Although he couldn't send such messages, he found protocols for contacting thousands of base and planetary administrative, corporate, and private organizations, even Earth Security. Some of these could only be used by the Captain and her most senior officers. Not surprisingly, Earth Security protocols were among them.

Without clearance, Len had no hope of directly contacting ES and little of chance of making indirect contact. Disheartened, he flipped aimlessly through the remaining information, seeing not the words but his mother desperately reaching for him. When finally she slipped back into memory, he was staring at the answer.

64 *Found by the Road*

Emergency signals.

The topic proved large, consisting of contingency after contingency and the appropriate channels for requesting emergency assistance in each case. Most required security clearance, but one special case did not: a general distress call. Only to be used in the direst of emergencies—misuse was grounds for execution--such a call could be sent by anyone in case cleared personnel were all dead.

Len flipped up the lenses and wondered if he could transmit that call without being caught.

Eight days out from Yellowknife, Fate handed him an opportunity, or the most he would likely get, when Kayla called him to the control center, a small, cramped pit in the heart of the ship aglow with computer displays embedded in the walls. "Bring your infospecs," she reminded him, although he was never without them. He found her standing like a marble goddess, intent upon the screens, her eyes obscured by her own infospecs. Len donned his and was instantly overwhelmed by a storm of information: objects, distances, socio-political data. A green line indicated their projected course. A blue line trailed back along their actual course to date.

He and Kayla were alone. The control center's staffing varied by situation. At its busiest, it would be crowded with navigation, flight, environment, and weaponry crew. Other times, it could stand empty.

"Let's review our approach," Kayla said.

He wondered how she knew he'd arrived, but then he realized she was annotated on his infospecs. He winked at the icon floating by her head and was presented with her name, age, height, weight, and job assignments.

She started talking before he could explore further. She led him through planetary approach, orbital injection, and descent. She pointed out issues with the existing plot and, while not letting him adjust any-thing, asked his recommendations. She praised his good calls and cor-rected his bad ones. Once she laughed and said, "That's double zero for sure!"

"Double zero?"

"You crashed us, bud."

Len bit his lip in embarrassment.

"No worries. Guess how many times I double zeroed my first time out?"

He shrugged.

"Fourteen. My mentor said sixteen, but he was wrong."

The lesson continued. Descent proved more tedious than the rest combined, and Len's mind drifted. He studied the control center in-stead, soaking up every detail his infospecs provided: panel layouts, con-trol procedures, available virtual interfaces. When he discovered a small communications console tucked in a corner, he examined it in detail. The emergency beacon was there, a red circle protected by a translucent cover. It could be operated manually or virtually. Instructions related how to record a distress message, virtually remove the cover with a blink, and activate the beacon with another.

Len hesitated. He couldn't do it without Kayla knowing, and he was pretty sure of her loyalties. If he did this, his life would be forfeit.

Just as his parents' lives had been.

"Hey," Kalya said. "You listening?"

Was it right to follow them into oblivion? He wanted justice. Revenge. What would they want of him? Or for him?

She snapped her fingers in his face. "Control to Len, Control to Len. Come in, Len!"

He drew a breath. "Sorry."

"What's wrong?"

"Nothing. Just, there's a lot of stuff here."

"Don't let it distract you. Not on final approach. That's double zero for sure." She smiled, her eyes mischievous.

"Sorry," he repeated. But his mind was no longer on the work. Would his parents want him to sacrifice himself? What had Kayla's parents wanted? Were they part of the crew? If not, what had happened to them? "How long have you been here?" he asked.

She flipped up her infospecs and cocked her head. "Since I was twelve. Why?"

"How did it happen?"

She didn't answer.

Len flipped up his lenses, too. "Complicated. I know. Did you have a choice?"

She shrugged.

"Why do you stay?"

Kayla approached so close he could feel her breath. He flushed with embarrassment. "Nowhere else to go. This is my family now. So're you."

"Some family. When we get to Yellowknife, what happens? Do people die? People like our parents?"

She drew back in surprise. "Hell no, Len. I told you, Captain has a deal with them."

Suddenly angry, he snapped, "Like what? Hand it over and nobody gets killed? That's almost as bad!"

"Of course not! It's a fair deal."

He turned away. How could she expect him to believe that? How could *she* believe it? This was a pirate ship!

"Damn, Len, you got a lot to learn." She took him by the shoulders and turned him around. She held on as she spoke. "We protect places like Yellowknife. They don't stand a chance without us. Without Anna Grande, Alexander Padgett would own it, and he sure would kill to get it."

"Who?"

Kayla flipped down his lenses. "Look him up."

He did. Padgett proved Earth Security's second most wanted pirate, more ruthless than Anna Grande though less cunning. Although rivals, the two had sometimes formed brief alliances. As with everything in the world of piracy, their relationship proved complicated.

He looked up Yellowknife, too. Although small, it played a key role in rim colonization as the most remote supply outpost capable of significant output. Father out, settlements remained small, barely self-sufficient, and of interest to none but explorers and renegades. Earth Security had been hard-pressed to provide adequate protection so far from home, which left those territories vulnerable to piracy. Ironically, Anna Grande offered stability. She was generally welcomed by the inhabitants, which vexed Earth Security no end.

"I don't understand," Len muttered. "If she does so much good, why's she at the top of the ES list?"

Kayla flipped up both their lenses. "That's one simple thing," she said. "Captain hates Earth."

"Why?"

"They killed her family. Swooped down from the skies one day, and…" Kayla gestured an explosion.

Len stared at her. He heard Cranmore's voice in his head: "She's just like you." Had Anna Grande seen herself in that frightened, broken boy lying in the rubble?

"There was a war on my planet, too," Kalya explained. "People died. I lost my home. My parents. My grandparents. My brothers. Everyone. Anna Grande found me. I'm here 'cause I asked to be."

She flipped down Len's infospecs and then her own. "Enough syrup. Back to school, kid."

Len stared at the navigation display. "Yeah," he murmured. "Back to school."

Reunion

Just payment for a good deed, Commander Len Vandermeullen groused. Kneeling on the cold steel deck, magnetic cuffs binding his hands behind his back, he eyed the smashed infospecs lying before him. He'd stupidly blundered into this, but how could he have known? The distress call, the damaged spacecraft, the cloud of leaked hydrogen—it was all *real*.

His patrol crew—pilot Jiang Mei, gunner Chike Danjuma, and technician Sara Mamani—knelt alongside him in a row, bound, blinders over their eyes, confined within these scorched, bloodstained walls. A killing hold. He'd led his people into a pirate trap.

A wiry young man and a severe older woman, a mother and son perhaps, stood guard. Vandermeullen might once have called them family, so he knew the drill: head down, mouth shut, wait for death.

Boots clopped up before his face, black, narrow, pointed, glowing in the harsh light. Vandermeullen waited for the inevitable. Would it be the crack of skull-splitting energy or barked demands?

Neither. "Leave this one. Lock up the others."

He knew that sharp alto voice. A glimmer of light momentarily pierced his gloom. The pirates dragged the other captives to their feet and rough-handled them out, leaving Vandermeullen alone with the woman. In the silence, she grasped his chin and tugged his face upward.

"Holy hell. Look who rode to my rescue."

Falling into her dark eyes, he was nine years old again, crawling from the rubble, blinking into a younger version of those eyes. His parents lay crushed beneath the stones as Anna Grande, the most notorious of pirates, took his hand and unofficially adopted him.

"Lenny," she said. "I never thought to see you again. Look at you. An ES patrol commander. I should spit on you." She pulled his chin up until his neck hurt.

"Your Majesty." She'd once quipped she was queen of the universe. He'd called her that thereafter, long ago.

Grande released him. "You remember that much." She tapped a device on her belt. The shackles clicked open and clanked to the floor. "Get up. You look ridiculous down there."

Rubbing his wrists, Vandermeullen rose. Although he stood half a foot taller than Grande, she towered over him in presence. Notwithstanding, she'd aged. Her light brown hair, hanging in tangled ringlets about her shoulders, was streaked with gray, and lines marred her lean face.

"You issued a distress call," he said. "Your hull is scored, your dorsal airlock is smashed, and you've lost substantial hydrogen."

"A scrape with a local patrol. It's nothing."

"So why the distress call?"

Grande circled, inspecting him head to toe like a drill sergeant. "Stories are flying around. ES patrols appearing out of nowhere, ambushing innocent ships, vanishing again."

"Pirate ships," he corrected.

"Tyrants use that word far too liberally." She stopped before him. "Padgett already tried to nab the tech."

Useful intel. Why had she let it slip? Next to Anna Grande, Alexander Padgett was ES's second most wanted. He'd been her ally on and off. Probably off at the moment. "Tried," Vandermeullen asked, "or did?"

She shrugged. "Did or will. I can't allow him toys I don't have. I want your stealth module, Lenny."

Vandermeullen laughed. "Really, Mom?"

"I could kill you and take it."

"You'd kill your son?"

Grande unholstered her sidearm and targeted Vandermeullen's chest. "You betrayed me."

"Growing up isn't betrayal."

"I saved you. I raised you for ten years, guided you from boy to man, and then you left, not just to strike out on your own but to become—" She motioned at his uniform, disgusted. "*This*. Fine payment for a mother's love."

Yes, she'd done all that. She also taught him order, discipline, even fairness, while her universe overflowed with chaos and cruelty. He knew why. She, too, had been orphaned. Her home, too, had been savaged, not by pirates but by Earth Security forces who unwittingly molded Anna Grande into their greatest enemy. While not as unprincipled as Alexander Padgett, she chose a lawless path, and in the end Vandermeullen couldn't reconcile that with the virtues she'd imparted.

Grande circled again, now a vulture. "I know your standing orders, *every* ES officer's standing orders regarding me. You wouldn't have put us in this position if you truly loved me."

"Love isn't that simple."

Her eyes glistened with incipient moisture. She blinked it away. "Your stealth module. Now."

"What do you know about it?"

"Enough." She pressed the barrel of her weapon to his heart.

"Removing it without computer verified authorization from the ship's commanding officer triggers a destruct mechanism. Killing me won't work."

Stone-faced, Grande pressed harder. "Killing your crew might."

Vandermeullen threw her words back at her. "You wouldn't put *me* in that position if you loved *me*."

"According to you, love isn't that simple." She touched the comm device on her collar. "Bring the prisoners."

Momentarily, Vandermeullen's crew knelt shackled beside him, their eyes still covered. Grande allowed him to stand unbound as she pressed her sidearm to Jiang Mei's temple. The young woman's jaw quivered.

Grande's eyes bored into Vandermeullen's. "Your decision, Commander."

He met her hot gaze with his own.

He did what he had to do.

Chike Danjuma watched the pirate ship fire its engines and drummed his fingers on his weaponry console. "We should destroy her, Commander."

Wearing a fresh pair of infospecs, Vandermeullen studied Grande's trajectory and reviewed the log of communications passing among nearby ES ships. "Her life for ours. She got nothing else. Stealth modules don't function without activation codes, and quantum tech can't be reverse engineered."

"But they're pirates, sir," Sara Mamani objected. "That might have been Anna Grande."

Jiang Mei shuddered.

Flipping up the lenses, Vandermeullen watched the ship vanish to a dot on the viewport. "Forty-three percent of pirates are women, people, and we're out of our jurisdiction."

"But sir…" Danjuma began.

Vandermeullen stopped him with a sharp glance. "Back to our patrol area."

He flipped his infospecs down. When Anna Grande kicked in her hyperdrive, her vessel's stats vanished from the display.

Falling Man

The only thing Reese Calhoun thought as he slid over the edge of the roof and plummeted toward the concrete was, "There goes summer!"

A moment before, he was repairing shingles on his three-story house in a neighborhood tall with time-honored oak and sycamore. Then a slip, and nothing between him and the driveway but air that whistled in his ears for two and a half seconds before he struck ground with a sickening smack. Somewhere, a woman screamed. Feet pounded up the driveway. Voices yammered around him.

"Oh my God!"

"Are you okay?"

"Is he dead?"

Reese drew a breath and sat. "Whoa," he muttered. "*That* shouldn't have happened."

The near-disaster had drawn five neighbors. One was the gray-haired lady across the street whose name he didn't know. Two were from the house on the right—John, he thought, and his teenage son John Jr., or maybe Jim and Jim Jr. He never could remember. And of course the couple from the house on the left, the Mazurs, Adam and Laura, he tall and beefy, she short and lean but made from case hardened steel.

"Lie still," Laura commanded. "You probably broke every bone in your body. Adam's called nine-one-one."

Logically, she had to be right, but Reese felt fine. No pain, no soreness, no lack of mental clarity. Ignoring the gasps and protests of the others, he stood and bounced on his toes, testing strength and balance.

"I'm fine," he decided.

Adam Mazur traced the line connecting the roof to the driveway with his index finger. "What, did you suddenly become Superman?"

Reese shrugged. "I think I'll go in," he said. "I could use a drink."

The ambulance screamed up the street before he could take the first step. Following questioning and a cursory exam by the paramedics which revealed no injuries, Reese declined a trip to the hospital, and everyone but Adam lost interest and left him in peace. "I'll have a drink, too," the big man said. He wouldn't take no for an answer.

"Let's be clear," Adam said around a sip of apple juice. (Not the drink he'd expected, but it was only nine thirty in the morning.) The two sat next to each other at the kitchen table while Reese's wife Penny, pecking at her laptop's keyboard and casting irritated glances their way, struggled with a term paper for a marketing class she was taking. "You fell forty feet, hit the driveway, and didn't even break a fingernail."

"Seems so," Reese agreed.

"That doesn't happen."

"Well, it did."

"People who fall that far onto concrete go splat."

"Not this time."

"Which means…" Adam poked Reese in the shoulder and nearly knocked him out of his chair. "…you've got superpowers, bud."

Reese downed the rest of his juice. "Or incredible luck."

"We've got to figure this out. Were you bitten by a radioactive raccoon or struck by acid rain or—"

"Adam."

"What?" Adam finished his juice and held out his glass for more.

With a sigh, Reese picked up the bottle and poured. "Don't be stupid."

"This kind of power is a gift and a responsibility. You've got to use it to help people."

"What he's got to do," Penny groused, "is call a roofer. I told you not to go up there, Reese."

Reese took his glass to the sink and rinsed it.

"Let's test the theory," Adam suggested. He guzzled half a glass.

"I'm not throwing myself off the roof again," Reese said.

"Of course not. We'll start small. Jump off the sofa."

Penny glared at Adam. "No jumping on the furniture, children."

Adam ignored her and finished his liquid refreshment. "Come on, Reese. I have a better idea." Leaving the empty glass on the table, he made for the door.

Penny raised both eyebrows at her husband.

"Maybe it'll make him go away," he muttered.

She shook her head and resumed her work.

A flight of six concrete steps led up to the porch. At Adam's suggestion, Reese stood on the third step and sprang to the ground, expecting to sprain an ankle. He didn't stick the landing, but it was painless. A flying leap from the top step produced the same result. So did a plunge from the roof of his pickup truck. And from a thick branch fifteen feet up the old oak in his front yard. By then, Reese was starting to believe in superpowers.

Adam had never doubted it. "You need a cape," he opined. "And a name."

"I have a name. It's Reese."

"Reese is your secret identity. You need a superhero name."

"Like what?"

Adam's face scrunched up in possibly the most intense concentration of his life. "Falling Man," he said.

"I think I'll call that roofer now," Reese said.

"You don't like it?"

"No! It's stupid!"

"Superhero names always are," Adam informed him. "So long as they're descriptive, that's okay. So, what does Falling Man do?"

"Falls, I suppose," Reese said. "But what's the point in that?"

"I mean what does he do to help people?"

Reese didn't care to guess.

Adam looked disappointed. "Simple. He does jobs with high risk of falling. Like rescuing people from burning buildings, or—"

"Or fixing their roofs."

Desperate to find some wrong for Falling Man to right, Adam motioned Reese to follow, and they walked down the street together until, two blocks down, they found a house overhung by a huge sycamore. Fifty feet up, a dead branch stretched precariously over the roof. Adam grabbed Reese's arm and pointed.

"Look! Catastrophe waiting to happen! Falling Man to the rescue!"

Adam crosses his arms over his chest. "Falling Man isn't bonded and insured."

They argued long and loud enough that the homeowner emerged to berate them for disturbing the peace. Adam explained that his friend, the superhero Falling Man, was here to remove the threat to the man's house, free of charge. Since the price was right—and it got the duo to stop fighting on his doorstep—the fellow agreed. He provided an extension ladder, rope, and a chainsaw, and was content to watch Falling Man endanger life, limb, and his customer's home while performing feats of superhero bravery.

Only once Reese was in the tree did he give much thought to how he allowed himself to be talked into this. But since he was already here, he supposed he may as well get on with it. He'd seen trees dissected before and knew how it was done, in theory. He cut up the branch in sections, using the rope to secure and lower each chunk to the ground.

He completed the job in short order, then lowered the chainsaw on the rope. All that remained was extricating himself from the tree. Naturally, he stepped wrong, missed the ladder, and plummeted while Adam grinned and winked at the terrified homeowner.

But Reese barely felt the impact. Picking himself up, he snarled something the other men fortunately couldn't hear.

"That's why he's called Falling Man," Adam told their customer.

The other shook his head in dumbfounded amazement.

Thereafter, Adam kept Reese busy, touring the neighborhood looking for odd jobs too high and dangerous for mere mortals. Reese removed deadly branches, fixed every roof but his own, and rescued a little boy who'd climbed twenty-five feet up a tree before realizing he was terrified of heights. Eventually, Reese didn't bother with ladders when coming down. He jumped, landed on his feet, and walked off with an air of smug self-satisfaction.

But pride goeth before a fall, sometimes literally. As the sun dipped to the western horizon, Adam landed Falling Man's final job of the day, untangling a bunch of helium balloons from a rusted television aerial that should have been removed decades ago. The lady of the house clapped with joy as the unsightly balloons drifted away on the breeze then watched in amazement as Falling Man jumped from the roof…

…and landed in a tangled heap, groaning and clutching his left wrist. When Adam tried to help, he got screamed at for his generosity while the old lady called nine-one-one.

This time, Reese accepted a ride to the hospital. Adam called Penny to give her the bad news, then went home, leaving her to retrieve him. She didn't rush. She arrived as the emergency room doctor was giving Reese discharge instructions. She offered to sign his cast when they got home. The doctor smiled, mistaking her sarcasm for a good bedside manner. When he was free to go, Penny helped him hobble to the car and strapped him in. Settled in the driver's seat, she said, "I guess those superpowers didn't work out, huh?"

What could he say? She wouldn't believe him anyway. So he just smiled at nothing and shrugged. If nothing else, he'd learned how to fall gracefully.

Bird Feeder

The girl—Tyler Martin thought of her that way, although she probably crossed the thirty-year line not long ago—spent most mornings out in her yard, so long as neither rain nor snow nor ice pelted the land. Fog she didn't mind, like this morning's fog, through which she glided over the grass, her jeans faded to gray, her blouse bleached of color, a sleek beauty of a ghost patrolling her haunt, her right hand dipping into the bag she carried in her left and flinging its unseen contents in a wide arc.

Tyler didn't know her name, but he fancied he knew her. He'd watched her through the picture window of his suburban ranch home for seventeen months—ever since Cassie stormed out and never returned. The girl reminded him a bit of Cassie, with raven hair spilling over her shoulder blades and that delicate, expressive face sculpted by a master artist.

She lived directly across the street from him in a house not unlike his own. Most homes in this neighborhood of gridline streets were about the same: small, linear, white. The girl's house broke the monotony with pale blue trim and a lemon-yellow sun stenciled on the front door. Her smallish yard was splashed with shrubs and flowers in haphazard arrangement, with one great red oak towering over the house in the back yard. Tyler could make no sense of her landscaping: no straight lines, no graceful arcs, just dots all about the place interspersed with a few shepherd's hooks from which hung an assortment of bird feeders.

Tyler watched her broadcast fistfuls of seed, watched her set aside that bag and take up another, watched her fill feeders emptied by birds and squirrels. A mysterious vision in the fog, she would have been more beautiful still in the clear morning light, when her pale skin glowed in the sun.

For seventeen months, Tyler had lived alone. It seemed the girl did, too. It didn't seem to bother her. She looked so happy out there feeding the birds. For his part, he was tired of living alone.

If only he could find the nerve to cross the street.

"Tyler?"

Startled, he looked up from the paperwork he hadn't been doing. He'd been hiding in it, daydreaming. That was the worst part about the promotion he'd received two months before: it cut into his daydreaming. He'd worked at the grocery store for almost seven years, first as a cashier, then stocking, then in customer service. He'd proven himself to the store manager, but lately his thoughts weren't on the job. They scampered out the door, scurried home, and up to the girl's door and that golden sun stencil. They rang her doorbell, waited impatiently for her to answer, and when her smiling face appeared, they ran through a hundred different greetings. None seemed quite right, so he backed up again and again, trying every conceivable variation.

"Hi, I'm Tyler. I live across the street."
"Hi, I'm your neighbor Tyler. I live across…"
"Hi there! My name is Tyler and…"
"Hey beautiful. I'm…"
(Oh God, she'd slam the door in my face!)

"There's a lady up front wants to talk to a manager," Aubrey said.

With an inward sigh, Tyler stood. "Okay."

She followed him with her wide, brown eyes and her hesitant smile. She always looked at him like that, like she was on the verge of asking him for an autograph.

At the desk, a wrinkled, gray-haired lady with a package of cookies in her hand glared at him. Her harangue began before he had a chance to say hello. Her voice broke over him like a ten-foot wave. He could only wait while the foam rushed up the beach. And while he waited…

"I couldn't help but notice you live alone."

"Do you live here by yourself?"

"I live just over there. I'm single. Are you single?"

Don't be an idiot. You can't start that way.

"Hi, I'm Tyler, and…"

"Are you *listening* to me?"

Tyler smiled stupidly at his customer and then at the cookie bag. It gaped open while she squished it in her tight grip and rattled it for emphasis. "Broken! Every last one of them! Well?"

He refunded her money and told her to keep the crumbs. She waddled off, a smug grin on her face, pleased to have beaten the establishment.

"I noticed you live alone. Me, too. Would you like to have dinner sometime?"

Aubrey came up beside him and watched the woman go. "You're just so calm," she breathed. "I'd have, well, I don't know what I'd have done." She looked up at him, eyes as wide as ever, and smiled. "You're amazing."

"Hi there. I live across the street…"

When he had a day off, Tyler watched the girl all day long, or rather he watched for her. Okay, she couldn't be in her front yard every minute of every day, but he checked whenever he passed the window, whenever he took his yappy little mutt Sulu for a walk, whenever he could find any reason at all to pass through the living room and peek across the street.

Sometimes he didn't see her for hours. Other times, he caught her feeding birds, weeding flower beds, or just sauntering, soaking up whatever she saw. Sometimes she wandered her own yard, other times she made a circuit of the block. Her mode of dress varied from day to day and even from morning to afternoon to evening. He'd see her in jeans and t-shirt, skirt and blouse, occasionally a short dress in which she looked particularly beautiful. She favored yellow and green clothing, but when she planted flowers, she painted broken rainbows with them. She hung out finch socks and woodpecker bars, suet and seeds, and tossed peanuts for the squirrels. With all the creatures that visited her—avian, insect, and mammal—the place looked like a scene from an old Disney flick.

The girl had no routine, or none that Tyler could divine. She came and went at random, except when she circumambulated the neighborhood. Those excursions took place most often Monday or Wednesday evenings. That gave him an idea, although it took him three weeks to pluck up the courage to execute it.

All Wednesday at work, he steeled himself for the task. Neither Aubrey's fawning over him nor irate customers snapping at him deflected his resolve. At home that evening, he prepared and watched, Sulu's leash in hand. At three minutes after eight, the girl slipped out, locked up, and glided down the sidewalk. Tyler called Sulu and clipped on the leash.

He waited until the girl had traversed half the block, then man and dog ventured in the opposite direction. Tingling all over with nerves and excitement, Tyler forced himself to take it slow and steady. *One step at a time,* he told himself. *Don't rush. She won't rush. She'll notice things—flowers, trees, birds. She'll stop, look, touch, smell. Meet her on the back side of the block, let her notice Sulu first. Women like dogs. She'll love Sulu.*

He rounded the corner, lost in anticipation, seeing nothing, feeling only Sulu straining at the leash, urging him faster, faster, faster! He almost gave in but forced himself to slow as he turned the next corner.

And there she was, at the far end of the block.

He stopped dead, unable to breathe. Sulu yipped in complaint and pulled him forward. The girl didn't notice. Sauntering by the neat little houses with their neat little yards, she bent down here to sniff a flower, paused there to touch a leaf, stopped elsewhere to listen to a bird singing on a branch. Time seemed not to exist for her, or maybe space had warped itself into a bubble surrounding her.

Tyler let Sulu pull him forward, all the while struggling to recapture the words he'd rehearsed. But they had no sparkle, no power to enchant the girl as could a flower or a bird or even an insect. What could he possibly say to her?

And then they were together, standing before the same green lawn, the smell of fresh-cut grass enveloping them, a bed of hyacinths spread at their feet, the branches of an old plum tree shading them, and he still lacked for words.

She smiled at Sulu and bent down to scratch behind his ears.

"Aren't you a handsome fellow," she cooed. "What's your name?"

Sulu about melted and pushed close for more.

"Sulu," Tyler said. His throat was so dry, he was sure he'd croaked the word. "I'm Tyler."

"I've seen you." She took Sulu's face in her hands. "Walking this guy. Looking out the window."

He felt like a stalker but couldn't even offer an apology. His voice had abandoned him. How stupid she must think him.

The girl rose and looked to the sky. Tyler's gaze didn't follow. He was drawn into her sparkling hazel eyes until she pointed upward. He reluctantly looked but saw nothing.

"That's your whole problem," she told him. She poked her finger at the sky again. "Didn't you notice? The moon playing peek-a-boo with us among the clouds?"

Puffs of cumulus and a smattering of cirrus floated over the face of the quarter moon, now hiding it, now revealing its edges, now helping the man in the moon's one visible eye give a conspiratorial wink. Tyler felt it urging him to make a move.

"What's your name?" he asked.

"What should it be?"

"Venus," he breathed, then wondered why he'd said such a stupid thing. The man in the moon winked again.

The girl laughed. "So, you do see, but only what you want to see. Alas for you, I'm married."

Her words stung like a slap to the face. "You can't be."

"Can't I?"

"You live alone."

"So, you don't see what you don't want to see. My husband works out of state. He comes home on weekends."

"I never seen him," Tyler objected, as though that would make this alleged husband evaporate.

"He doesn't waste time mowing the lawn while he's home. We run off. To the beach. To the mountains. To our room." She started on her way again. When he didn't immediately follow, she motioned him to accompany her. He hurried to catch up, then their shoes tapped together along the sidewalk, slow, steady, until she paused and pointed to an old maple across the street.

Tyler looked at her instead. Her eyes sparkled in the sun.

"Look at the world," she insisted. "Not at me."

"You are the world." But he reluctantly looked where she indicated. A trio of squirrels chased each other up and down the trunk, through the branches, higher and higher as though they intended to climb all the way to the moon. Far above the tree's crown, a hawk glided on the thermals. Back on the ground, a rabbit scurried across the yard to the safety of a thick rose bush.

The girl smiled at Tyler. "See? You're not hopeless after all."

The hawk wheeled and soared north until it diminished to a dot and Tyler lost sight of it. He had a strange urge to follow, but he knew he could never keep up, and anyway what would be the point?

"You never know," the girl said, "unless you *do* follow."

Had he voiced the thought? He was sure he hadn't. "Are you psychic?"

She gave him a gentle nudge. "Don't be silly."

"Then who are you? How can you know my thoughts?"

"Open your eyes and your ears and your heart, Tyler. Observe. Listen. Ponder. It's not that hard."

The rabbit came out of hiding, hopped to a juicy clump of grass, and nibbled on the blades. Tyler watched for a time before saying, "I'd really like to know your name."

But the girl had slipped away like a passing cloud evaporating on the wind. He stared at the spot where she had stood as though he might find her hiding in plain sight. She didn't materialize. Finally, he tugged at the leash and said, "Come on, Sulu."

Man and dog completed their circuit of the block alone together, stopping every so often to sniff a flower or study the clouds or enjoy the antics of the squirrels.

At the end of his shift on Thursday, Tyler asked Aubrey if she'd like to have dinner with him. She could barely contain her joy. He took her to a nice Italian place, where they ate and talked for an hour and a half. By the time he dropped her off at her place, he knew it wouldn't be their last outing.

He got up early Saturday morning and watched from his window. About seven thirty, a car backed out of the garage across the street. He stepped outside just before it pulled away and waved to the girl and her husband.

They both waved back, and she and gave him a playful wink.

In Plain Sight

This could be dicey. I'd avoided Yumi for three and a half weeks by traveling to New York, Atlanta, and Chicago, discreetly seeking appraisers, potential buyers, hiding places, but now I was back, and she demanded a meeting that I had neither excuse nor courage to refuse.

When her instructions arrived by text the moment I debarked the plane Friday evening, cold dread overtook me:

Tomorrow. Noon. Sheldon Park. Bench by the playground. Bring the books.

A more reckless man would have already sold them and vanished on the proceeds, but she knew me. I took my time and did my homework. That's why I was her top operative. Ironically, it now proved my undoing. Sold one at a time, her books would have provided a comfortable retirement; sold as a collection? Visions of wealth danced in my head. Thus the trip, the appraisals, the quiet search for a buyer. My instinct proved right. The take was so high, the numbers hardly mattered. The trick was completing the sale without drawing attention, a feat still in the works. And now here I was, Saturday noon, the loot in my hands, about to lose it all.

A treasure like that, and she wanted me to hand-carry it through a public park? Well, of course. She always hid her secrets in plain sight. Take Yumi herself. Seated on that park bench, she looked like a mother enjoying the summer day while her children played. Warm sunlight reflected—or did it emanate?—from her yellow dress. A gentle smile graced her glowing, round face, while her small hands cradled a white clutch bag in her lap and stroked it like a cat. You couldn't help but look. She'd ignore you, of course, lost in the antics of the kids at play.

You'd hold your breath or smile at her, her serenity, her beauty, her happiness, hoping maybe for her to notice you and smile back, but lost in her, you'd never realize that among the white, black, and Hispanic children swinging on swings and sliding down slides and brachiating across the monkey bars, not one looked remotely like her, not one the smallest fraction Japanese.

She was no child's mother. That fact stared you in the eyes, but you'd never realize. You'd never guess the darkness within.

I came to her side, a doubled and tied plastic grocery bag in each hand, a baker's dozen books in one, a common man's dozen in the other, none visible to the passerby. She had eyes only for the swinging, running, squealing children, so I settled the bags beside her and sat next to them. A light breeze rustled our hair, hers jet black, mine sandy. A glance at her, a slight twitch in her smile, told me what she was thinking.

Oh, Christopher, you're such a gentleman.

Sarcasm, of course. I a robber of the rich, she an empress reigning over thieves and thugs, and this transaction but to avoid unpleasantness. As valuable as they were, I should never have stolen those books. I should never have allowed myself to notice them. In true Yumi fashion, she had stored them on a shelf lined with fakes. Print books had faded into oblivion, inflating the value of those that remained, but as décor, book-lined shelves never became passé. Few noticed the difference. None who did dared take them. None but me. I knew Yumi, knew her ways, knew my own skill. I fancied she'd never suspect me.

Yumi touched one of the bags and shook her head. *No, Christopher,* I could almost hear her say. *It wasn't that. You're too full of yourself. You must prove yourself smarter than me. Smarter than a woman.*

Maybe so. If so, she'd torn a gaping hole in that hot air balloon. I knew who I was up against. I planned this job more carefully than any in my life. I'd disabled the surveillance, allowed no witnesses, left no evidence, conjured a perfect alibi. Even a clairvoyant wouldn't have pinned it on me, yet somehow Yumi knew.

I would have to live with that failure, if she let me live, but the pain of a crushed ego quickly gave way to a worse agony: I, Yumi's right-hand-man, would be turned out, *persona non grata*, to make my way on my own. I had grown up in her organization. I had nobody apart from her and her people.

Especially her. In that moment, I realized I loved her. Not in a romantic sense, but in some convoluted fashion bordering on religious. I couldn't lose her and live.

Yumi looked down as though embarrassed by my realization. She probably had known it long before. Maybe she even felt something in return. She opened her clutch and took out a small object, an item so perfectly her it nearly made me laugh: a rare Captain Hook Pez™ dispenser that she'd bought for over a thousand dollars. She slipped a candy from the dispenser and with an elegant little toss popped it in her mouth. Her eyes misted over. She watched the children. The candy dissolved. She ate a second candy, then a third, while working out what to say, or rather to signal. She wouldn't say a word. Not here. Not now.

She turned, hesitant, a tear in the corner of each eye, and held out the dispenser to offer me candy. I opened my palm, and she dropped a piece into it.

I'll miss you, too.

Her whole being broadcast it. It was the truth, unspoken but undisguised. With a nod, I closed my fist around the treat and stood.

The truth, yes, but not the whole truth. Without looking back, I passed by a trash barrel, dropped the candy in, and left. I didn't need to see her to know her thoughts.

Beautifully done, Christopher. You're not smarter than I, but you're damn close.

Maybe, maybe not, but I knew her. She hid things in plain sight. And I had no stomach for poison.

Olly Olly Oxen Free!

Cobwebs and spiders notwithstanding, the best hiding place in the house was behind the broken wall in the basement. Marty *never* looked *there*.

Mason wormed through a breach barely big enough for a spaniel, gingerly tucking aside silver spiderwebs, and put his eye to the ragged hole dad's hammer had accidentally punched in the drywall two years ago. From there, Mason could see the unfinished treads descending from the kitchen and the shadowy forms of the furnace, water heater, and laundry machines. A bare bulb hung extinguished at the foot of the stairs.

Overhead, his sister Marty called, "Twenty-nine! Thirty! Ready or not, here I come!" Her feet thumped across the floor.

He chuckled. She'd *never* find him.

"A great concealment, indeed," another voice agreed in his ear.

Mason almost squealed in fright. He clapped his hands over his mouth as hot breath pulsed over his shoulder.

"But Father cautioned you against playing down here, did he not?" Long, cold fingers raked his hair.

Mason wanted to run, wanted to scramble out and fly up the stairs, but his legs had turned to stone. Shaking, he shifted his eyes toward the voice but saw nothing. "Who…" The word froze on his lips.

A finger tickled the line of his jugular. "Guess."

Vampire, he thought but could not say.

"Hmm," the voice equivocated.

A sudden light flashed through the hole in the wall and little feet hammered down the wooden stairs. "Come on, Mason!" Marty whined. "I give up! Olly olly oxen free! Olly olly oxen free!"

"Arr!" the voice whispered. The fingers shrank from the light. The hot breath blew away. "Stupid children! What nonsense is this? It's 'All ye, all ye, come in free!'"

A white eyeball glistened from the other side of the hammer-hole.

Mason screamed.

Marty laughed with glee. "Found you!" she cried.

Count to Ten

The black cat shot from the Kowalczyk's hedge across my bow like a cannonball. At the same instant, the crack of a bat sounded, and ten-year-old Brian Kowalczyk nearly beaned me with a line drive hit off his younger brother Steve's pitching. As Steve scrambled after the ball, Brian grinned sheepishly and waved. "Sorry, Mr. Stevens!"

After my years in Nam, I don't startle easily, and anyway, no harm had been done. I waved back and said, "Nice hitting! Who's cat was that?"

Brian shrugged and took a practice swing as Steve scampered back to the imaginary mound, ball in hand.

I'd never seen a black cat in our neighborhood, so it was either a stray or somebody's new family member. I should know. Every afternoon, I did a half-hour march around the area to keep my heart and my doctor happy. This had been my routine since my wife passed away two years before, and along the way I talked to people, so I knew everyone, dogs and cats included.

Then again, it was October thirty-first. Maybe somebody had planted that cat to scare me.

Okay, not really, but the thought was amusing. Leaving the baseball game behind, I walked on, enjoying the Halloween decorations in the windows of the near-identical split levels, the jack-o-lanterns by the doors, the ghosts fluttering from tree branches, the plastic gravestones standing in the lawns. The sun burned in the clear autumn sky. The kids would have a great night for trick-or-treating.

Oddly, when I came to the end of the block, that black cat was waiting for me. Or no. This one was bigger with a white locket on its breast. It eyed me as I slowed, smiled, and said, "Hi there, little—"

It bolted down the sidewalk, then turned and glared at me.

Fine, I thought. *Be that way.* Still watching it, I reached the curb. Just before I stepped into the street, it charged me and strafed my feet. At the same moment, a sky-blue SUV streaked by, blasting the neighborhood with sonic vibrations presumably regarded by the driver as music. Stunned, I watched the vehicle vanish down the street. The cat bounded after it before ducking into Mrs. Golino's daylily beds.

I had a momentary urge to follow and see if it belonged to the Golinos, but no, that wasn't possible. Mr. Golino loved to regale folks with stories of his allergies: dust, tree pollen, peanuts, goldenrod, and cat dander.

So where had it come from?

No telling. I looked both ways three times before crossing the street. Down the next block, I saw Paul Twenebo perched on an extension ladder, lopping dead limbs off the big maple in his front yard. The tree had already dropped most of its foliage, but a few red leaves clung to it. Wearing goggles and attacking the wood with a hand saw, Paul looked sinister, like he'd stepped out of a horror movie. Downed branches littered his lawn.

I would have called a greeting but didn't want to startle him. Two near misses were enough for one day. He heard my footsteps, though, and as the next branch fell, he glanced back and waved. "Hey, Mr. Stevens! Ready for trick-or-treating tonight?"

"Laid in half a ton of candy," I replied.

As he laughed and returned to his work, I caught movement in a smaller tree on the opposite side of the walk. Before I could react, a skinny black cat leaped from the yellowing foliage and all but landed on my shoulder. Startled, I twisted out of its way and lost my footing. As I fell, a yelp sounded above, and Paul tumbled out of the tree. He spilled onto the walk a few paces ahead. His ladder and saw crashed between us.

I scrambled to my feet. "Are you okay?" I asked, hurrying to Paul to help him up.

"Whoa," he said. He stood and brushed off his knees and examined his palms. "I sure hope the missus didn't see that. She didn't want me up there in the first place."

"What happened?" I expected him to say the cat tried to kill him, but he hadn't seen it.

"I guess I didn't have the ladder placed right."

The demonic beast was nowhere to be found, so I didn't mention it. Once assured Paul wasn't hurt, I went on my way and noticed, with a backward glance, that he had repositioned the ladder and returned to the fray. Brave man.

But me, I was starting to go nuts. Everywhere I looked, I saw sinister cat eyes peeking from the bushes. Can you blame me? Three black cats, on Halloween, each precipitating a near-disaster! This wasn't just coincidence. It was an ambush, a coordinated attack. Where was the next one hiding? In a tree? In a flower bed? Around the corner of a house? Inside an open garage? Under a car? I kept my eyes peeled for any sign of unusual activity, any movement in the shadows, but saw nothing. Unfortunately, when you expect an assailant hiding nearby, you readily miss the one waiting in the open.

Which the stout black cat with the white rear paw was. It strolled by innocent as a child as I was passing Martin Couture's excessively fertilized, emerald green lawn. I didn't notice it until it rubbed against my leg. Sucking in a sharp breath, I nudged it away with my foot. "Scat!" I commanded.

It didn't scat. It purred, circled me, and rubbed against me so persistently friendly that I halted to avoid stepping on it. And that's when the attack came. A little red sports car zipped by and fired a hubcap at me. The disk spun across my path, barely missing both the cat and I, mowed a great arc across Martin's lawn, spitting grass tips as it went, careened into Mrs. Wilson's yard next door, and struck her garden gnome, nearly decapitating it. Plaster dust sprayed everywhere. A moment later. Mrs. Wilson exploded through the front door, screaming. She rushed to the gnome and ran her hands over the poor, injured thing. Then she screamed at the retreating car, "Get back here! You break it, you buy it! Don't you dare run off!"

But it squealed around a corner and was gone. The cat, of course, vanished before I could finger the real culprit.

"Did you see that?" Mrs. Wilson wailed at me.

"Almost got hit by it," I told her.

The way she stroked the statuette, she probably wished I'd thrown myself in front of the hubcap. I didn't bother explaining that soldiers aren't called to sacrifice themselves for plaster gnomes.

I had to finish my exercise without dying, if possible. I moved on, twice as alert now, mistrusting every leaf rustling in the breeze. I took extra care rounding the next corner. No cats, no cars, no vans, nothing. All quiet on the western front.

Until an explosion of spitting and hissing broke the silence. Black cats five and six racketed by, embroiled in a feline turf war. They chased through Mrs. Sasaki's columbine and ferns like enemy pilots engaged in a—pardon the cross-species metaphor—dog fight until, tangled in a hissing ball of black fur, they rolled over my feet. Mortified, I stood as still as a military statue but looking rather less heroic until they charged back through the ferns and vanished. Just as I breathed a sigh of relief, a mud dauber, one of those incredibly stupid wasps that sting if *they* fly into you, zipped by my nose. Clearly it was in league with the cats.

I had to escape this onslaught. I had to get home, lock the door, and pull down the blinds. I picked up my pace and wished I had brought my gun with me. Somebody needed to teach these monsters a lesson!

Expecting more cats to pounce at any second, I narrowly missed the big green beach ball that sailed in front of me and into the street with little Ruthie Sorenson racing after, oblivious to everything else. As it sailed by, a huge black cat materialized from nowhere, shot passed her, and slammed into my ankles. I went down hard, right in front of Ruthie, who spilled over me, wailing and stretching her tiny arms in vain as a passing F150 ran over her ball.

Somehow, the ball escaped unharmed. I helped Ruthie up. "Stay here," I told her. "I'll get it for you." I kept watch for more cats or vehicles until I was safely out of the road and the ball restored to the child. "Why don't you play in your back yard?" I suggested. "That way the ball can't get run over."

She nodded solemnly and, sniffing and hugging her ball, trotted off. As I watched her go, a strange notion took root. No longer obsessed with cat attacks, I became lost in thought and, without realizing it, reached the end of the block and stepped into the street.

A sleek black cat flashed by my feet, forcing me to stop just as I heard the squealing brakes. A white Chevy rolled by while its driver, a young woman dressed all in black, cussed me out. In a daze, I wondered if she was a goth or just done up for a Halloween party.

I stumbled on. The world, I mused, was far stranger than I could have imagined.

I was two doors from home when the ninth black cat crossed my path at an easy pace and yowled like a ghoul. The sound froze my blood. I stared after it as it passed by, until something struck the sidewalk with a strange clatter. Now what?

I picked up the object. Ice. A hailstone the size of a golf ball. I looked up. The sky remained that crystalline October blue. Where had *this* come from? And how had the cat known?

Didn't matter. My strange notion was right. The cats weren't attacking me. Maybe something else was after me, but not them. They were protecting me!

I reached my driveway to find one last black cat sitting there, having a bath. It looked up at my approach and yawned. I bent down and scratched it behind the ears. "So what are you here for?" I asked it.

It blinked at me.

I supposed I would find out soon enough. I started for the front door.

The cat mewed gently.

I looked at the animal.

I looked at my front door.

A whiff of rotten eggs seeped from a window.

I turned and went the other way, paid Mrs. Kowalczyk a visit, exchanged a few pleasantries, and asked to use her phone. Then I called the gas company and told them to get out here before my house blew up.

Good kitty.

Christmas Future

It's rough being me.

First, I have to go around in *this* getup. Black doesn't suit me. I'm more of a shimmery, barely-there sort of guy. My person, I mean, not my clothing. Without this bulky black cloak and monk's hood, you'd probably think I was a hallucination. My form constantly shifts, see, like the future.

But no, I can't go around like that. The Boss has this dress code, at least for me. So instead of intriguing people, I'm doomed to scaring the dickens out of everyone.

Dickens.

Never mind. Bill Murray was right about that joke.

So anyway, there was this guy, let's call him Chuck. You know those people who say live for the moment? Chuck wasn't one of them. If someone handed him a million dollars, he'd put it in the bank and boil pinto beans for dinner. Not that he had money. He'd blundered into a copy editor job with a local newspaper, not a lucrative position, and stayed there. On top of that, he was a lousy date. How many girls want to eat boiled pinto beans while watching reruns with their guy?

Yeah, Chuck's life and prospects were pretty miserable, facts which somehow escaped him. Finally, the Boss figured Chuck needed shaking up and sent me in. Aside from the cloak, that's the thing I hate most about this job. I can't have encouraging chats with clients over cups of coffee. No, I have to scare the…

Forget it.

I materialized in Chuck's living room that Christmas Eve, right behind him, because sneaking up on people is so effective, and tapped him on the shoulder.

He looked at my huge black form and empty black hood and said, "Hi, Bob. Didn't hear you come in."

Yeah, this was going to be tough.

Sprawled on a battered green couch, he was watching *M*A*S*H* reruns on a twenty-six inch TV and eating an American cheese sandwich on cheap white. Dry. Yuck.

To get the ball rolling, I pointed at the TV.

"Have a seat." He rolled out of his sprawl and patted the sofa. "Want something to eat?"

My hand, when it extends out of that black cloak, appears rather skeletal. I've no idea why, but it's scary. Waggling it in front of his face, I pointed again.

"You've lost weight. Want some peanuts?"

I'm not allowed to speak. Another of the Boss's strange rules. I can only direct my subject's attention. It usually works, but not everyone is quick on the uptake. Sometimes it takes several tries. I thrust my finger at the TV for emphasis.

He squinted at me. "What's up, Bob? Why are you dressed for Halloween?"

Fine. He'd asked for it. With a sweep of my cloak, I enfolded the entire room in darkness. Then I spread out a terrible vision. It emerged in a swirl of gray mist that slowly lifted to reveal an old man lying on that same green couch, all alone, still watching *M*A*S*H* reruns, breathing his last. His eyes glazed over. His chest stilled. His cheese sandwich slipped from his limp fingers and flopped on the floor.

"Whoa," Chuck whispered.

I pointed at old, departed Chuck. I pointed at the still living version. My bony fingers waggled between them to suggest, "Get it? That's you if you don't get off that couch and *do* something!"

"Is this like virtual reality or something? That is soooo cool!"

I've dealt with some dense customers, but this guy was clearly a moron.

As a second warning, I conjured him losing something more appealing than his life. Another swish of the cloak and another scene emerged from the fog of the future. And was she gorgeous! A buxom, raven-haired beauty sitting on Chuck's lap, arms draped over his shoulders, smiling at him as he munched on his sandwich. He stretched to see the TV beyond her wavy locks. What an idiot.

"We could go to the movies," she suggested.

"This is more cost-effective," he countered.

"There's that new seafood place downtown." She pulled him close and kissed his cheek. "I'm famished!"

"Too expensive. I got stuff if you're hungry."

The lady shoved him away. "Damn it, Chuck, I want *real* food! I want *real* entertainment! I want you to pay attention to *me*!"

Chuck waved her off. "Shh. This is my favorite episode."

She slugged him in the face and stormed out.

Present-day Chuck watched his jilted doppelgänger probe his bleeding, broken nose. "That is soooo realistic! How do you do this, Bob?"

Admittedly, I broke the rules. But hey, I was seriously irritated, and that's putting it mildly. So I spoke. Okay, screamed. "I'm the Ghost of Christmas Future, you moron! I'm showing you what will happen if you don't get your act together and get off that couch!"

Strictly speaking, I wasn't. I made that stuff up. I have a good imagination. But he couldn't know that.

Chuck chuckled. "Yeah, right. C'mon, Bob, tell me how you do it."

I left. If I hadn't, I'd have broken his worthless neck.

Oddly, in spite of my complete and utter failure, in spite of trashing the rules, the Boss told me I'd done a fine job. He even said he'd gotten a laugh out of it, which is pretty high praise. He loves a good joke. But honestly, I couldn't see how I'd made the slightest difference.

Only years later did I catch up with Chuck again. He was a changed man. He'd gone back to school, studied technology, and become a hot name in the virtual reality gaming world. He'd created a series of blockbuster hits based on the *M*A*S*H* TV series. (What else?) More astonishing, he'd married this buxom, raven-haired beauty who was the marketing genius responsible for his games going viral.

As for me? I'm still here, doing the exact same thing. How depressing. Sometimes I think I need a visit from myself.

Fireworks at Midnight

The booming music, the roar of voices, the swirling lights and bodies and party hats and screaming noisemakers...too much! He had to escape!

The big boss, CEO Maddox Carlton, towered over everyone at the far end of the room, his back to the bar, drink in hand, laughing, joking, waving expansively with his free arm. He looked like a GQ cover in his perfect blue sports coat and perfectly styled black hair and devilish mustache. Everyone nearby paid him rapt attention, for he was simultaneously host, guest of honor, and star of the show. He had summoned everyone in his employ, no exceptions, here to greet the new year, to celebrate a successful launch, to gaze into a future that held even greater things, guaranteed.

A great night for center of the world Maddox Carlton but not so much for insignificant technical writer Fred Hollins, who hated crowds, hated noise, and especially hated showoffs. The venue irritated him, too, this exclusive waterfront hotel such as he could never afford to set foot in, not even to buy a candy bar from the vending machine. He even hated the drink in his hand, which was guilty by association. He set it on a table and pushed through the crowd, not bothering to beg anyone's pardon, and slipped into the shadows at the side of the room to sulk.

But that proved no escape at all. The tidal wave of noise engulfed Hollins and dragged him out to sea to drown. Even with eyes closed and hands pressed to his ears, the roar penetrated his bones. Giving up, he surrendered himself to the tsunami.

He wasn't the only one it swept off. At a dim table by his side, a thirtyish woman picked at a plate of nachos, not quite eating them, more likely sampling for poison if the look on her face meant anything. *She must be a kindred spirit*, Hollins thought.

She knew he was watching; she pointedly looked the other direction, out the window to the beach.

Hollins nearly recognized her. She worked in accounting, maybe. Or not. He couldn't match a name to her heart-shaped face and dark hair. Wondering what she saw in the night, he looked out the window, too. The ocean beckoned, whispering he should leave, come to the sand, come to the shore, escape to that tree-lined cove he knew and loved where he could mark the passing of the year in his own way. The night was perfect for it, more perfect even than last year.

But what about the woman? Did she have an escape, or was she stranded? It would be heartless to walk out on her. Not that he could suggest it, probably. She'd get the wrong idea. But he couldn't leave her to drown. Could he?

"Hi," he said before he knew he was saying it.

"Bye," she replied.

"Horrid party, isn't it?"

She swirled a corn chip in cheese sauce and half-heartedly scooped up a chunk of tomato.

"I'm Fred. Fred Hollins."

"Who cares?" She popped the chip into her mouth.

"Would you like—"

"Nope."

"But I didn't even—"

"No need. I don't want a drink. I don't dance. I certainly don't care to celebrate a non-event with obnoxious buffoons. Let me eat my dinner in peace."

Hollins couldn't see how nachos qualified as dinner.

"This is the part," she said. She took a sip of her drink. It looked like water: no color, no fizz, no nothing. "Where you hit on someone else."

The verbal slap pushed his injustice button. "I'm not hitting on you, damn it. I'm rescuing you."

The woman raised an eyebrow without looking at him.

"We both hate this." He motioned around. "I'm leaving. Come with me."

"I'm not going home with you, or to a hotel, or anywhere resembling a bedroom."

"I didn't suggest it."

"You thought it."

"I didn't."

She ate another chip, plain.

Give up, Hollins told himself, but he'd never been good at taking advice. "You know what I do at midnight on January first?"

"Do I look clairvoyant?"

"Fireworks."

She took another sip of her presumed water. "Fireworks bore me."

"Not rockets' red glare fireworks. Real fireworks."

That, at least, got her to look. Her brown eyes glimmered in the pale light, laughing at him. "You start a forest fire, maybe?"

"Forget it," he grumbled. "Stay here. Bore yourself to death. I'm leaving." And so he did, shoving aside anyone who got in his way. Nobody noticed. He left the party room, stormed down the corridor to the lobby, exchanged his claim check for his coat, and hurried into the cold, clear night. He was halfway through the parking lot when he heard her voice.

"Paging Mr. Fred Hollins. Please meet your party by the filthy Chevy pickup with the broken taillight."

He turned. The woman approached wearing a light blue blouse, a knee-length denim skirt, and a heavy black coat, unbuttoned. Odd getup for a midnight party. "I'm such a good target," he guessed, "that you couldn't resist insulting me further."

"Collecting on a debt. You promised me fireworks."

He figured it was the only apology he'd get, so he capitulated. "Follow me."

She buttoned up and accompanied him to the edge of the beach where he turned west and led her away from the lights and the cacophony spilling from the hotel. They walked twenty minutes and more with the stars overhead and the waves splashing on the shore. A stand of trees loomed before them, dark and foreboding, but he knew a path through and before long they emerged on a quiet, sandy spit of land. In the dark night, the sparse grasses and the sea and the shadowy forest suggested a world newly created just for them.

"Here we are," Hollins said.

The woman took it all in, pirouetting in slow motion. "So we are. And the fireworks?"

"Up there." He pointed to a swath of bright stars. One brilliant diamond sparkled in its midst, silver, blue, yellow, silver, red, silver, blue, orange, silver.

He heard her hold her breath.

"Well?" he asked.

"I've never seen such a star before."

"Sure you have, every clear winter night. You just never noticed."

"What is it?"

"Sirius. The dog star, the eye of Canis Major, the brightest star in the night sky."

Lips parted in awe, she watched it scintillate. "Why bring me here now?"

He smiled at the star and her and the star. "It culminates—reaches its highest point in the sky—at midnight every New Year's Eve. Watch and you'll see."

She tried. "I don't see anything. The sky moves too slowly."

"No, it doesn't. Come here." He led her down the shore, closer to the trees. There, a branch reached out over the water. "Stand so Sirius is behind that branch. Hold very still, don't move at all, and watch."

Sirius crept westward and upward, its movement all but imperceptible, yet within a minute it had full risen above the branch and sparkled silver, blue, silver, orange, blue, silver, red, silver. It took but a minute.

"Amazing," she breathed. "You *can* see the sky turn!"

"Not the sky," Hollins corrected. "The Earth, carrying us along."

She tottered a little as though she could feel the Earth spinning beneath her feet.

Hollins pulled his cell phone from his pocket and opened his atomic clock app. The red display counted down the final moments to midnight, measuring out hundredths of a second as they watched the Earth shift within the arms of its mother, the cosmos.

Midnight came.

"There," he said.

Beyond midnight now. Sirius dipped, gliding westward, until it vanished behind the branch once more. Another minute later, it peeked out below, shining silver, yellow, red, silver, blue, silver, orange, yellow, silver.

"Fireworks," Hollins told her.

"Real fireworks," she agreed.

"Shall we go back?"

"Why? The show's only started."

He was glad she understood. Not everyone would. "What's your name?"

She laughed. "Who cares? What's yours?"

The fireworks had probably blotted it from her memory.

He didn't mind.

Rush, Rush, Rush

The golden-haired woman threaded through the airport crowd, pulling a cherry red suitcase which bumped and squeaked behind her, protesting her Olympic speed. Reaching the travelator, she hit the conveyor belt without breaking stride and kept left to pass the sluggards letting the machine do all the work. She overtook other walkers, too, calling, "Excuse me! Excuse me!" as she came upon them. They stepped aside to let her pass.

All but one.

Moseying along, that young man glanced back and stopped dead like he'd either met the Grim Reaper or the love of his life. The woman knew and loathed that look, but before it registered, the slack jawed fellow dropped his black case smack on her sandaled foot.

She yelped and, hopping on one leg, waggled her injured toes. "What the hell!"

"Oh, damn," the man sputtered. "I didn't…are you…God, that's a beautiful shade of green!"

She tentatively tested her foot's load bearing capacity. "Black and blue, more like!"

"Your nail polish." He nodded at her feet. "It's amazing with that dress, and your eyes, which are amazing, too. You're not married are you? What's your name?" He bent down to retrieve his property.

"Medusa," she snapped. "Avoid my eyes and get out of the way." She scowled at his case, a black box with a handle and a row of knobs along the top.

"Avoid a vision like you?" He looked so serious she wanted to punch him. Maybe he realized it, because his interest shifted to the knobs on the box. He fiddled with them as though the device might teleport him away.

Her instincts told her to push by and be done with it, but she couldn't contain her curiosity about the object with which he'd attacked her. If nothing else, the information might prove valuable if he'd broken her metatarsals and needed suing. "What *is* that thing?"

"Amplifier," he said. "Just a little one, for practice sessions. What's your real name? Mine's Jack Wasserman."

"I don't care." She tried to move on, but he smiled with such hope that she felt an urge to take him home and feed him some kibble. Okay, that wasn't fair. He was a handsome guy. Dark, wavy hair. Angular face. Toned biceps. A roguish glint in his...

Stop it! she scolded herself. The last time she let a random stranger's good looks seduce her, it cost her twelve hundred dollars plus an emotional upheaval tax.

"Please?" Jack pleaded. "I can't write a love song about a girl named Medusa. Oh, I probably could, but it wouldn't end well, and I could use a happy ending."

"You're a broken-hearted song writer, huh?"

"Song writer, anyway. Guitarist. Up and coming superstar."

"And modest." Braggarts she could do without.

"A guy can dream, can't he?" Jack smiled that winning smile again.

She didn't get how a guy could drop an amp on her foot one second and fall hopelessly in love with her the next, but the incongruity warmed her, while that look in his eyes left her light-headed. Her cattiness embarrassed her. "Simone. Kluftinger."

Jack's eyes widened. "You've got to change *that*! It doesn't suit someone so elegant."

He could have just slapped her. "Simone is *very* elegant, jerk."

"I meant that last name. Simone Kluftinger sounds like someone running Simone through a blender. But Simone Wasserman, that's music."

"*What?*" He couldn't be proposing, not at first sight, not after attacking her, not on a travelator of all places!

She must have had her mean face on, because Jack put up a hand to fend off a blow. "Don't be upset! I'd like to get to know you, that's all. Are you in a hurry?"

Hurry was Simone's middle name, or that's what her mother always said. "Simone can't go less than ninety miles an hour," Mom liked to quip. "The only reason she doesn't have enough traffic tickets to build a house is the cops can't catch her." But rushing was merely habit, not necessity. Or maybe genetics. Or fear of interacting with idiots like Jack Wasserman.

She should have said she was late for boarding. Alas, lying wasn't among her talents. "Sixty-three minutes, which doesn't leave much time for writing."

The sparkle in Jack's eyes suggested his inflated opinion of her kicked up a notch. "What do you write?"

"Horror."

"Sell any?"

"Not yet, but a woman can dream, can't she?" She felt stupid repeating his line, but oddly, saying it brought insight: she understood Jack better than she cared to admit. Always rushing toward some imagined destiny, they both missed what was right in front of them.

Jack's smile told her he knew her secret, too, but she didn't dare let him know that she knew he knew. "This has been great, getting my foot smashed and all, but I really must go."

He put a gentle hand on her shoulder, a familiarity for which she would have slugged anyone else. "Come on, Simone. You have at least half an hour to waste on me. How about it?"

She wanted to. She didn't want to. She looked ahead and saw the end of the travelator drawing nigh. Jack still faced her, oblivious to the end of their ride.

That suggested a solution to her dilemma.

"I suppose my resolve could break," she said.

"I'll keep begging. On my knees if I have to."

The belt dipped into the floor. Jack hopped from the travelator without looking, simultaneously taking her hand and helping her off, all as smooth as magic.

"How did you do that?" Simone gasped.

"Musician," he said, tapping himself on the chest. "Practiced sense of timing. How about it?" He nodded to a nearby sandwich shop.

He was still holding her hand. Strangely, she didn't mind. "On one condition," she said.

"Name it."

"I read you the first chapter of my novel, and you tell me what you think."

He readily agreed. Although, a few other customers left in disgust once Simone got started. Not everyone, it seemed, liked vivid horror stories with lunch. But Jack ate it up.

Entanglement

"I can't go up there, Helen."

My wife looked at me over the white rims of her glasses. The gold flecks in the temples glinted in the late morning sun streaming through the window of our spare room. "I don't have time to handle everything myself, Gib. Most of it is yours, anyway." She resumed sorting through the pile of papers, tossing most of what she found into a box for shredding and recycling. "I don't know why you kept any of it."

"You do so."

The attic was my version of this room, a dumping ground, only here cast-offs had been stashed in case they were wanted later: boxes of photos, piles of fabric Helen had never used, stacks of old magazines, cartons of tax returns and legal documents. Above the ceiling, leftovers of a different sort slumbered, memories I dared not revisit. I hadn't been up there in eighteen years.

"Then you're better off rid of it. Be quick and don't rummage. You'll be done in fifteen minutes, half an hour tops."

"You could hire someone to do it."

She thumped a thick folder into the recycling box then brought me a box of trash bags. Pressing it into my hands, she kissed me on the cheek. "Sometimes we need to prove ourselves to ourselves. Go. Fifteen minutes, Gib, that's all it will take."

Terror slept in that attic, a spaghetti bowl of entangled memories. At fifty-three, I had squirreled away as many as any man of similar age but with a difference. Mine threatened to engulf me. That's why I never revisited them, why I had cut myself off from the world. Unable to socialize or hold down a job, I hid in our isolated home in the north-west Illinois hills while Helen became my fortress, not only supporting me but securing my isolation. Forcing me to confront the past felt like a betrayal, but I went through with it. She had done so much for me. Maybe I owed her this.

Trembling, I opened the hatch, unfolded the ladder, and climbed into the cramped, unfinished space. With an early summer noon approaching, the air smelled of warm wood and cobwebs. Shapes lurked in the dim: old boxes shut for years, a few bags stuffed with the unused and mercifully unremembered, a makeshift rack on which hung clothing both worn and pristine. *Be quick,* Helen had said. *Don't rummage.* I was and did not. The sealed bags went first, grabbed by the drawstrings and tossed without ceremony down the ladder to the floor below. Then I opened a fresh trash bag and addressed the clothing that hung in the open.

All of it had to go. Shirts, pants, coats. I took each by the hanger and stuffed it into the trash bag, barely looking, touching as little as possible. Where sight triggered memories, touch could seal my fate. So many memories were woven into each sleeve, spilled onto each cuff, stuck like dog hairs to each collar. I worked as quickly as caution allowed, coming last to my old black wool coat.

It proved too powerful. Lifting it by the hanger, careful not to brush my fingers against its smooth fabric, I found myself pulled into its blackness anyway, and in the blackness gray shadows swirled. Laughter tickled my ears. The scent of pine needles filled the air.

"Stop shaking it and open it!" my mother laughed. Her eyes sparkled. I shook the gift one more time to tease her. Beside her, my father laughed, too. My younger brother and sister sat cross-legged on the floor, itching for me to get it over with so they could tear into their next presents. By the picture window, the Christmas tree shimmered and sparkled.

My girlfriend Krystal, seated on the couch next to me, said, "I'll do it for you if you don't hurry up!" She tugged at a corner of the wrapping paper.

"Oh, no you don't, this is mine!" I tore into the brilliant gold and silver paper, then opened the box within. My breath caught in my throat as I tugged the black wool coat from the box. It was the most elegant coat I'd ever seen.

"Put it on," Krystal insisted, and I obliged. It fit perfectly. As I turned to give the gathering the full effect, she added, "You look like a movie star!" Everyone agreed.

She loved that coat as much as I, more even, and everywhere we went that winter and the following winter, too, I wore it for her. She hung on my arm and whispered in my ear that we were the perfect couple, that everyone admired us. I didn't know about that. I just knew I wanted to be with her forever and hoped the coat would last that long, too. It felt like a part of us.

In January of that second winter, we traveled across the state to Chicago for a rock concert. As luck would have it, an arctic blast assaulted the city that same weekend, but we didn't care. Full of bravado as we approached the venue, I unbuttoned my coat, pulled Krystal in, and wrapped us in it. She laughed as the wind bit into our cheeks. "Glad we came?" I asked.

She snuggled against me, the delicate scent of her floral perfume teasing my senses. "I'm always glad to be with you, but you should have ordered better weather."

"I tried. The weather bureau wouldn't listen."

"Usually you're more persuasive, Gibson." She kissed me, slipped her hand into my coat pocket, and pulled out our tickets. "Shall we?" She handed them to me.

Releasing her, I rebuttoned my coat and took the tickets. When I looked at them to check the seat numbers, I discovered everything wrong. The date, the location, the event name, nothing matched up. "What the hell? Krystal, did you—"

She was gone. The cold was gone. Chicago itself was gone.

Wrapped in the warmth of the attic, coat in one hand and tickets in the other, I read the print again. Madison, Wisconsin. Two weeks from now.

Damn.

Breathing hard, I shoved the tickets back into the coat's pocket, balled up the garment, and stuffed it into the trash bag. I yanked the red plastic drawstrings and tied them in a double knot. After throwing the bag down the hatch, I sat on a carton, shaking uncontrollably, and buried my face in my hands. I could still smell Krystal's perfume. It had been her favorite, especially in summer. She wore it every day during our August road trip that year, so as it wafted toward me on the hot air, I knew without looking that she'd emerged from our motel room in her red and yellow bikini to join me by the outdoor swimming pool. I waited, reclining on the lounge, pretending not to notice, until she slipped into my lap and draped her arms around my neck.

"Look who finally showed up," I teased.

She kissed me. "Should I go back inside?"

"Absolutely not." Taking her in my arms, I tucked her in beside me. Her skin, soft and tanned, still felt cool from the room's air conditioning.

She didn't resist but joked, "Don't get *too* frisky. People are watching."

"Yeah? Like who?" The lounge creaked as I shifted and rolled her beneath me.

She fought just a little but yielded in the end. "Like the whole universe."

No, they weren't. We were the only ones there. Even the parking lot was deserted that afternoon. I took her face in my hands, kissed her, and nearly told her so, but then she wasn't in my hands anymore.

Sitting on the attic floor next to the open carton, I found its innards spilled before me—postcards, letters, travel brochures, receipts. In my trembling fingers, I held a piece of motel stationary. On it a single word had been written.

Goodbye.

I could still smell her perfume lingering on its fibers.

Double damn.

Tears stung my eyes. I wiped them away on my sleeve and crunched up the paper. Then I gathered up the spilled litter and the box it came from and stuffed it all in a new trash bag. Somehow, her final note wouldn't be discarded. Each time I shoved more of the past into the bag, that note stuck to my hand and returned to me, refusing burial. I knew I shouldn't, but in the end I had no choice. I uncrunched it and read it again.

Please come.

Helen clumped up the ladder. "How's it going, Gib?" She could tell the moment I looked into her eyes. Swallowing, she turned away and started back down.

"Helen?"

Her footfalls paused.

"I'm going to Madison."

"What, today?"

"In two weeks."

The silence was so deep she might have vanished.

After that, I rushed through the rest of it. I saved nothing, touched as little as possible, almost didn't breathe. Once the refuse of my life had been bagged and hauled out to the garage to await trash day, I found Helen in the kitchen picking at a tuna sandwich and staring out the window. I sat beside her. The bread, mayo, and tuna were still on the table, so I made myself a sandwich, too, although I wasn't hungry.

"I'm sorry," Helen told the window.

"Me, too. I shouldn't have saved any of it."

"I shouldn't have made you do that."

We were lying naked on the bed, Leiah and I, her pale skin glowing in the dim light. I stroked her cheek and shrugged. "You didn't make me."

"Then why did you?"

I didn't know. I loved Krystal. We were happy. I wanted to be with her forever. Yet here I was in the sack with another woman. Utterly stupid and senseless. "Lust, I guess."

"She'll find out, you know. Women always find out."

"Not always."

Leiah pushed me away. I watched her rise and dress. "She will. I know. I've done this before."

"Done what?"

"Seduced guys like you. Attached guys. I hate myself afterward, every time."

"Then why do it?"

"Envy. Your girlfriend—what's her name?"

"Krystal."

"Krystal. Lucky, lucky Krystal. I met her the other day. God, I hate her, the way she gushes about you. It feels good to pull a woman like her down a peg or two. Gives a worthless girl like me a sense of power." Finished dressing, she retrieved her purse from the chair and went to the door. "At the time, anyway. The guilt comes later, and the jealousy always returns. If it's any consolation, you were good."

It wasn't, and ultimately Leiah was right. Somehow, Krystal found out. She never explained how. She only left that one word.

"You don't know?" Helen had my hands folded in hers. "Then maybe you shouldn't go."

I looked into her soft brown eyes, brushed her dark hair back behind her ear, and sighed. "I have to. Entanglement."

She peered into my eyes, sympathetic, searching. "Do I come with you?"

I could foresee nothing, but I could guess. "No. But you'll be there anyway."

Unsure what to expect, I waited on the sidewalk in the cool evening while concertgoers filed in, talking and laughing. Nearly an hour passed. My tickets were long gone to the landfill with the rest of my cast-offs, so I wasn't going inside. Not that I cared to. I only wanted to finish this and get home before something else dragged me into the past.

I had about given up when I caught the familiar scent of her perfume.

"Gibson?"

I turned and there she was, eyes wide with surprise.

Krystal had aged so gracefully I almost thought I'd slipped through time again, but no. Her hair had lightened a touch, the skin about her eyes had stretched a tad tighter. Yet she was still beautiful. I wondered if I looked as good to her. Probably not. The years had taken a toll on me, emotionally and physically.

"Krystal."

"What are you doing here?" She came close and offered me her hands which I took in mine. Her touch was still light, her smile still infectious.

"It's good to see you again."

"Well…yes! Yes, it is, but…oh, this is strange!"

For a few moments, our eyes alone carried on the conversation. I felt her life pass before me and mine before her. I knew her joys and pains, and I knew why she was here. "Your son Jared is in the band."

Without releasing my hands, she stepped back in surprise. "You know him?"

"I know you." I pulled her close again, closer than before. She allowed it.

"Gibson, I…why are you here?"

Because, I thought, *you asked me to come.* "Why do you think?"

"All these years." She looked away, sad but not angry. "I was thinking about you the other day. I haven't in ages. I was at the table with my morning coffee, staring off into space, and there you were. I wished I could see you again." Krystal looked up. Tears glistened in her eyes. "And here you are."

"Here I am."

She stroked my face but looked confused. "You're married now. Helen, right? How could I know that?"

I pushed a strand of hair out of her face. People moved by us without paying us heed. "I wish I hadn't hurt you." It wasn't an apology, but it was all I could muster. Could apology even mean anything after all this time?

"Don't cling to the past, Gibson."

"It clings to me. Entanglement."

I didn't expect her to understand. Who could, unless they experienced it as I did? Yet she looked thoughtful as she regarded me. "Do you know what became of her? Leiah?"

I did. Threads of her life had imposed themselves on me for some years before they vanished into the mist. I didn't wish to burden Krystal with it, though. It wasn't a pretty tale. I shook my head.

"I've got to go." She kissed me on the cheek and tugged her hands from mine. "Will we see each other again?"

I shrugged. "I can't foretell the future."

We didn't say goodbye. Maybe that was a sign. She walked away and after one backward glance slipped into the theater. Alone again, I shuffled to the parking lot where I'd left my car. Strange. She had called, I had obliged, but nothing of value had passed between us.

Don't say that, I could sense her think. *Every encounter becomes part of us, changes us, entangles us.*

Undeniably so. The good, the bad, the beautiful, the ugly, it all creates our now and points toward the future.

Sometimes, Helen had said, *we need to prove ourselves to ourselves*. Maybe I had done that, maybe not, but it was time to stop dreading, time to stop hiding. If I could. For the moment, I was exhausted. I just wanted to get home to Helen.

Maybe together we could figure this thing out.

Stuck

It was pitch black and raining and they were stuck somewhere in the West Virginia Appalachians, not moving, when Connor closed his laptop in disgust because his story, set during a rainy, pitch-black night in the West Virginia Appalachians, wasn't at all moving.

He pushed his head against the headrest, closed his eyes, and insulted himself in a mumble so as not to wake the elderly gentleman in the aisle seat. Gentleman, he generously styled the fellow, although the guy looked borderline bum: tattered jeans and a wrinkled red plaid button-down shirt; a two day growth of stubble on his face; thin, gray hair in disarray; mouth hanging slightly open as he gently snored.

Outside, Connor saw only blackness spotted by dark raindrops trickling down the window. Whatever the holdup was, they'd been stuck here for over an hour. The lights in the train had dimmed long ago. According to his cell phone, which sat charging on the tray alongside his laptop, it was nearly midnight.

Midnight, the witching hour for writers, the hour when ghosts and demons, ancestors and angels came out to play. For him, anyway. Nothing written after midnight, he'd heard another writer say, ever had to be rewritten, and he believed it, in spirit if not always literally. But tonight shades and specters abandoned him, off haunting some other writer, stranding him in the graveyard, chilled, soaked, with no open grave into which to fall and write.

The elderly gentleman snuffled and shifted position.

Connor shifted, too, and reopened his laptop. On the screen, a blank word processor page taunted him. He set fingers to keyboard and sat, waiting, mind similarly blank. He typed a word.

It

He typed another

It was

How could he say what it was? He didn't even know what "it" was. Fed up, he typed the obvious.

It was a dark and stormy night.

He deleted that and reset his fingers to home position.

The elderly gentleman snuffled again. "Never start with 'it,'" he said.

Connor looked at him and found him wide awake, deep blue eyes searching Connor's face, thin lips stretched in a thin smile. His skin looked pale, almost translucent, in the light from the monitor.

"That's my personal rule. Never start with 'it.' Start with pain or pleasure, excitement or boredom, danger or..." He looked at the extinguished overhead lights.

"Safety?" Connor suggested.

"Nope. Never, *ever* start with safety. That's even worse than some amorphous 'it.'"

"You're a writer?"

The elderly gentleman took a moment to push himself up and right his seat. He wiggled about to get comfortable, then lowered his tray and set his folded hands upon it. "I, young man? A writer? Do I look like a writer?"

Connor started to wish the guy hadn't wakened. "Writers come in all shapes and sizes and—"

"And states of decay. Right. No, I'm not a writer. I just read a lot. Or used to. It's hard to find anything new that's worthwhile."

"That," Connor said, closing his laptop, "is because all the good stories are taken."

The other looked skeptical.

"It's true. What's your name?"

"What's yours?"

"Connor."

"Frank." Frank stuck out his hand.

Connor reluctantly shook. Frank's fingers were thin, skeletal, cool. "Okay, Frank. You read, so you know there are only seven plots, right?"

"I know no such thing."

"Well it's true. Look." Connor opened his laptop to do an internet search, but there was no WiFi on the train and no cellular signal at midnight in the rainy Appalachians of West Virginia. "Trust me on this," he said, closing the computer in disgust. "Seven or three or five or nine, depending on who you ask. The point is, every story has already been told ten million times before. So unless you're Shakespeare or Poe or Steinbeck or Bradbury, unless you're a genius, you don't stand a chance of even sounding new and worthwhile."

Frank scratched his cheek.

"Damn straight," Connor concluded and opened his laptop. That blank page was still there. He set his fingers to the keyboard and waited. Nothing happened, but at least the conversation was over.

Or not, as it happened. "Then why sit at a keyboard waiting for inspiration? Think you're a genius, do you?"

Of course he did, sometimes. "Of course not," he said.

"Huh. Well. Nobody's ever written *my* story, anyway." Frank pushed the release and leaned his seat back. He wiggled about to get comfortable in his new position.

"Your story?" Connor didn't imagine he had much of one, but he couldn't resist asking. "What's your story?"

Frank closed his eyes. "Not sure, but I'll know it when I read it."

In the distance, the train's horn sounded, muffled by the mountains and trees, and with a slight lurch they began to move. Frank's jaw slid open two finger-widths, and he snored gently.

Never start with 'it,' Connor grumbled to himself. *Hell with you, old man. I'll start however I like.* And so he began to type:

It was pitch black and raining and they were stuck somewhere in the West Virginia Appalachians, not moving, when...

Do Not Open

With every step, gray ash swirled about her legs. Flecks fluttered in the breeze, stuck to her clothing, dotted her face, drifted back to ground like alien snow. For ninety minutes and more, she walked, crawled, dug, and sifted in the charred ruin of the mountaintop building until the stuff caked her orange coveralls, transforming her into a smoky specter of someone once called Tara Kelly.

Tara took no notice. Her work consumed her. Important people were paying for answers. One answer in particular: what was this place before it burned? Nobody knew. The land belonged to a consortium of Maryland and West Virginia universities. Intended for an environmental research facility, land and forest remained untouched for six years thanks to ongoing budget crises. Or so everyone thought. Somehow, someone snuck a building onto the premises. It had remained undetected until the fire. Now, only two fragments of wall remained, joined in a rickety corner that creaked in the wind.

The fire marshal had passed judgement on the cause: an explosion triggered by faulty wiring. The big questions remained, and the universities wanted answers, so they called upon Tara Kelly's forensics investigations firm. Tara personally rode to their rescue in her bright blue pickup, toting her bag of tricks. She arrived with the sunrise and after four hours on site had nothing.

Nothing but the basics, anyway. The fire made a meal of nearly everything, and its meager leftovers told her little. Wood structure reduced to cinders. Fragments of warped, ablated metal so light she suspected titanium, testifying to the intensity of the heat. This had been no ordinary fire, so how had those fragments of wall survived?

Their empty window frames taunted her and drew her eyes to a door-way high up in one wall, serving what must have been the third floor.

The sight of that doorway reminded her of Jared. She looked away, trying not to let thoughts of him derail her work, but she couldn't help it. Would he be there when she returned home in the evening dark? Would his voice greet her, or would the house silently mourn his absence? She had tottered on the edge of that cliff all week, not knowing from day to day whether he would still be there, staring from their empty door into the night, hoping she would materialize from the darkness.

Stop, she told herself. *You have work to do.*

Tara crunched from interior to exterior. Here, the carpet of destruc-tion thinned. Given how few unidentifiable fragments of things remained within, likely none awaited discovery without, but she searched anyway, in part to avoid that inexplicable door a little longer. But soon it forced itself upon her. Hands on hips, she gazed up at it, eyes narrowed, mind churning.

It must have led somewhere. A fire escape, most likely, but that meant metal stairs, and only the pervasive ash and bits of charred wood littered the ground below. She sifted through the detritus once more to be sure, and this time found, buried deep, a slab of scorched metal.

A door bearing the shadow of a message, licked nearly clean by the flames: *Danger! Do Not Open!*

Tara envisioned this door twenty-five, thirty feet off the ground, leading from a comfortable office to certain death. It was so ludicrous, she nearly laughed, but a sharp sound diverted her attention.

The racket rose from the wooded slope to the north and infiltrated the burned-out clearing. Someone crashed through the undergrowth, whistling and smacking a solid stick against trees and rocks in passing. She held her breath as a pale figure tramped up the rise, and the whis-tling morphed into singing.

'Tis the flame of the hearth-fire bright
Light of friendship, heat of loving,
'Tis the flame of the hearth-fire bright
That draws us home a-smiling.

The voice might have been man's or woman's. It tottered on the dividing line. A male silhouette formed, tall and straight, lean and wrinkled. He came up the slope, head down, a mop of white hair crowning his head. He wore dark jeans and a dark plaid shirt that accentuated the paleness of his skin. His thin voice rang as clear as the sky as he made for Tara, his pace steady and unhurried, singing that chorus over and over as though he didn't know the verses.

She should have risen, should have hailed him, but fear turned her legs to stone as she watched his approach. Something about him looked wrong.

'Tis the flame of the hearth-fire bright
Light of friendship, heat of loving,
'Tis the flame of the...

"Oh!" he gasped. He stopped five paces off. His eyes sparkled green in the sunlight and had a sunken look, as though he hadn't slept in a month. Though Tara couldn't say why, he looked different, not quite human, as though his species had diverged from *Homo sapiens* a mere five thousand years before, or maybe after. "Oh," he repeated and looked about as though expecting an ambush.

Tara swallowed and rose. She brushed the ash from her coveralls, or as much of it as she could, and coughed as the dust settled.

The man held a sturdy walking stick in his left hand. He leaned sideways on it and gave her a crooked smile. The line of his mouth seemed excessive, and when his lips parted, he had no teeth, or none Tara could see. "Did I startle you? I'm sorry."

"No," she lied, but when he cocked his head she felt compelled to some degree of honesty. "A little. I didn't expect anyone. There's been a fire."

He peered at the ruin, at the walls, at the doorway in the empyrean. "That's an understatement. Blaze. Inferno. Conflagration. My English is good, yes?"

She heard no accent. She waited, but he didn't speak further. He just stared upward with his sunken, gray eyes and quietly whistled the tune again.

"What are you doing here?" she asked.

"Passing through. That's the phrase?"

"We're a dozen miles from the highway and there aren't any paved roads, just a few dirt tracks."

"But I'm walking, see?" He hefted his walking stick for emphasis and grinned.

"Yes, but…"

He slowly approached. Tara felt a rush of panic even though he made no threatening moves. He must have sensed her fear. He stopped and put up a hand. "I won't harm you. But we might as well stand close enough to talk in a normal voice."

That stick could be a nasty weapon, but she nodded. She thought she could probably defend herself against a frail, old man if necessary. Although, the hike up the mountain hadn't winded him. He might be stronger than he looked.

Now at her side, he frowned at the warning sign on the soot-covered door bedded down in the ash. "So. They knew."

"I'm sorry?"

He licked his lips and grinned with that unsettlingly wide mouth.

"You aren't just passing through."

"Oh…do you have a name?"

"Tara." She said it automatically then wished she hadn't.

"Tara." It rolled off his tongue like a smooth waterfall. "That's a beautiful name."

"And you are?"

"Nothing so elegant. You can call me—" His brow creased. "John Smith. Is that right?"

"If you have something to hide," Tara agreed. "I think you should leave. I don't need you trampling my evidence."

"Faulty wiring, wasn't it?" John Smith's smile was way too innocent.

"I'm not investigating the cause of the fire."

"Then what?"

"What this place was. Who built it. I don't suppose you know?"

"University property, isn't it?"

"Is that why you're trespassing?"

John Smith studied her as though she were an insect, then asked in a near-whisper, "Tara, have you ever—have you ever felt your life spinning out of control?"

She felt Jared's hand slip from hers, saw him walk out the door, wondered if he would ever return.

John Smith looked to the trees. "Yes, you know what it's like."

Tara flushed with anger. "Don't try to distract me. If you know anything about this—"

"*Distract* you? I'm explaining!" He shifted the walking stick to his right hand and shuffled through the ash to the charred wall. Tentatively, he touched it, ran a finger through the soot, studied the black mark it left on his pale, almost translucent skin. "Sometimes you must cut your losses, must walk out the door, leave everything behind, start anew. You have no choice but to walk through that door."

He lifted his eyes to the portal far above. "But when someone installs a door, you assume they know where it leads." He turned and gave her a pained look. "Was anybody hurt?"

Tara shook her head. No injuries had been reported, no human remains found. The building must have been empty when it erupted in flames.

John Smith sighed in relief.

"What are you running from?" She didn't understood a tenth of his words, but she sensed he knew what she needed to know.

"Execution."

"You're a fugitive. From where?"

John Smith gave Tara a sad smile. "No. That never happens where I come from. Retribution strikes like a falcon. I left before the falcon's eyes found me."

"What did you do?"

"What you do." He kicked at the ash and sent gray motes spinning through the air. "I asked too many questions."

He walked around the wall. Tara heard him scuffling through the debris. She thought to follow but had the strangest feeling he needed privacy, so she waited and listened to the soft shifting of ashes. When he returned, he held a small object clenched in his right fist. In his left, he carried a metal slab a foot square, flattened by pressure, blackened by fire. He set the slab gently at her feet.

"That should answer some of your questions," he said. "As many as are safe to answer."

"Where did you find that? I searched—"

"In the wall. I suspect my eyes are more sensitive than yours at certain frequencies."

He began to leave, but she stopped him with one more inquiry. "Who *are* you?"

He paused. Although she couldn't see, she thought he was examining the object he had taken from the debris. "A traveler," he said. "These days." As he vanished down the slope, his voice carried to her, singing lightly.

> *'Tis the flame of the hearth-fire bright,*
> *Light of friendship, heat of loving,*
> *'Tis the flame of the hearth-fire bright,*
> *That draws us home a-smiling.*

"From where?" Tara asked nobody. She picked up the metal slab and shook it. Something rattled about inside. The exterior bore no markings she could find, or none that hadn't been gnawed off by the flames.

She studied the doorway above once more. *When someone installs a door,* the stranger had said, *you assume they know where it leads.* She understood. Wherever he'd come from, he could no longer go back. Maybe he didn't care to, save occasional moments in the dead of night when he longed for home. Had he walked through a door of his own making, or had someone placed it before him and pushed him through? Had it been built there, wherever there was, or did someone here construct it, not knowing what lurked beyond?

Tara had unwittingly given Jared such a door. Her long hours on the job stretched too far into the night, too far across the weekends, an invisible barrier shutting him out. She'd poured so much into her company that she had nothing left for him. She hadn't realized where that door would lead. But maybe her door didn't open from a burned-out building onto empty space. Maybe if she kept the light on and the door unlocked, Jared would find his way back.

Metal slab firmly in hand, she returned to her truck, threw the object on the passenger seat, and started down the mountain. Much work remained, and she hardly knew the shape of it, much less the degree. As for the results, whatever was in there, it could mean big trouble for somebody. But all that was somebody else's problem.

She had a door to tend.

How Not to Camp

The whole problem, Rick grumbled to himself, was lack of procedures. Andy was in charge of this campout, but he proved seriously lacking in organizational skills.

Andy's first priority was pitching the tent, followed by starting a fire and cooking dinner. After that, as the sun set behind the western forest, they could drink and tell jokes and ghost stories and generally have a grand time. But where were they now, two hours after arriving at the campsite? Step zero. They hadn't even unpacked. And why was that? Paul had put it most succinctly: "How?"

Translated into plain English, the procedural requirements for construction and operation of wilderness living facilities had neither been properly developed nor documented, much less distributed to those parties with a designated need to know.

So here they were, a gang of government employees supposedly on a fun-filled team building excursion, reduced to writing campsite operational procedures.

Might as well have stayed at the office, Rich groused to himself. At least there, he'd had a chair to sit on!

Thirty Minutes of Evil

You are cordially invited, the note began, after which it turned devilishly hostile.

Batts thought it a brilliant piece of work.

You are cordially invited to be pummeled and cudgeled, dissected and disemboweled, exposed, mocked, spit upon, stoned—to play, in short, a starring role in thirty minutes of evil, accompanied by light refreshment, in my home at the above address this Friday evening. Festivities commence at midnight.

With warmth and sincerity,
Jerome Batts

P.S. Attendance is mandatory. Note your name publicly posted on the above website. Your sins will be appended in the event of your absence.

Please RSVP ASAP.

He emailed five invitations and within four hours received five replies. He read not a one.

Robinson arrived first, Phil Robinson, a lion of a man with a full golden beard and steel eyes that pierced you, accusing you of dreadful crimes you'd never committed. A man of power and wealth, owner of a successful chemicals company, neither given to nor accepting of stupidity. Contempt poured from him, probably even in his sleep.

"Who the hell are you," he asked, "dragging me into the middle of nowhere in the middle of the night?"

Socially, he surely meant, not geographically, for Batts had summoned his guests to a modest house in a modest suburb near the edge of a large city's sprawl, a locale generally unnoticed, yes, but not quite nowhere.

"Can I get you a drink?" Batts answered. A good half foot shorter than Robinson, he smiled up as though gazing at a star, hoping it might explode for his amusement.

"What've you got?"

"Water, with or without lemon or lime." When Robinson made a face, Batts said, "Afraid I sucked it from your factory's waste line? Confidentially, I did."

Robinson snorted, and Batts showed him to a battered green couch in a tiny living room. Along with a loveseat, a wing chair, and a recliner, the sofa crowded a circular coffee table where Batts had placed an open box of cheap sugar cookies. The room was dim, lit by a couple of inadequate lamps. The few paintings on the walls featured undraped figures. The love seat bore stains suggesting it had been used for an eponymous purpose.

The doorbell rang as the tycoon sat. "Bore yourself for a moment," Batts said. "I shall return."

At the front door, guest number two glared out of the midnight gloom. Kate Pollack, once upon a time splashed about the top glamour magazines, now owner of several, was wrapped against the cool in a turquoise dress and matching shawl, a forced frown on her plastic face. "What the hell is this about?" she demanded.

Batts bowed to her and with a sweep of his arm motioned her in. "It's all about you, of course." He led her to the living room and directed her to sit in the wing chair to Robinson's left.

Gardner and Emily Phillips, old, wrinkled, holding each other up on unsteady feet, arrived next, dressed formally as though posing for a donor portrait, an activity constituting their primary occupation. Their faces adorned brick walls in hospitals, museums, libraries, and a church or three. "Now see here," Mr. Phillips said. He might have explained what Batts should see had not Mrs. Phillips sputtered, "What the hell is this damned charade?"

"Just as you say, ma'am," Batts replied with a little smile. "It's hell. Do come in."

"Did you hear how he spoke to me?" the Mrs. asked the Mr., who nodded as Batts led the way to the living room and seated them together on the love seat. In the dim, their old eyes didn't notice the stains. They made, Batts supposed, a lovely couple, scowling there like that.

"Just one more," he told the gathering, "then we can—ah! There he is!" He answered the tolling of the bell and returned with a short, balding fellow, Pal Smythe, waddling behind him like a duck. Smythe could have done with more exercise. A lot more. He sputtered nonsense syllables at his fellow guests before bleating, "What the hell—why the hell—these guys?"

"Some of the guys," Batts informed him, "are girls."

"Women!" Kate Pollack snapped. Her jaws about snapped, too.

"Perhaps," Batts mused. "We shall see." He pointed Smythe to the recliner, completing the circle. "Before we start, would anyone like water, with or without lemon or lime? Or cookies?"

None, it seemed, had any appetite. "A shame," Batts said none too sadly, reboxing the baked goods. "They were, of course, poisoned."

Everyone yelled at once. He couldn't understand a thing they said, which suited him fine. Walking slowly in a great circle behind them to keep them nervous, he said, "Allow me to explain." That shut them up. "You all have money."

"I don't," Pal Smythe objected.

Batts smiled a thin smile. "Mr. Robinson owns a successful business. Ms. Pollack could assemble an extensive wardrobe from dollar bills stitched together. Mr. Phillips was born to money, which Mrs. Phillips cleverly married into."

"How dare you!" Mrs. Phillips strangled her own fingers and looked pointedly away.

"And Mr. Smythe, though he doth protest, is on everyone's payroll."

Terrified, Smythe put up a hand like a traffic cop and blubbered. Robinson peered suspiciously at Smythe. "Meaning?"

"Meaning," Batts explained, although not precisely, "he has significant disposable income. As do you all."

"So you brought us here," Pollack sneered, "to rub shoulders with the rich and famous?"

"Not at all, Ms. Pollack. I brought you here to flog you, to watch you writhe in agony, to savor delicious evil and be consumed by it. Surely my invitation was clear enough?"

"Speaking of enough," Mrs. Phillips said, rising. "I think we've all had precisely that." She looked at her fellow guests, but they avoided her eyes and failed to budge or agree. Their names were all posted online, and thus far only Batts knew how much he knew.

Batts circled 'round behind Pal Smythe and set a companionable hand on his right shoulder. "Tell her, Mr. Smythe, why she won't leave."

Smythe swallowed and craned his neck in a failed effort to show Batts his terror, to beg for mercy. Batts could feel the fear in Smyth's taut and trembling muscles. Digging his fingernails into the man's shirt and flesh, he insisted, "Tell her."

Smythe closed his eyes and whispered, "Mr. and Mrs. Phillips launder stolen art."

Batts maintained his grip. "Louder, please."

"Mr. and Mrs. Phillips launder stolen art!"

"Liar!" Mrs. Phillips screeched. Mr. Phillips grabbed her hand and yanked her none too gently back into the love seat. Seething together, they indeed made a lovely couple.

Batts released Smythe and slipped around the circle, stopping behind the duo. "Lying," he said gently, soothingly, "is surely evil. But it's your evil, Mrs. Phillips, not Mr. Smythe's, not in this instance. His evil is profiting from evil." He moved on, pausing behind Mr. Robinson, who for once tried to hide from the world, although the attempt was doomed to fail.

"Mr. Smythe," Batts prompted. "If you please."

Smythe covered his face in his hands.

Robinson pushed himself up, or would have had not Batts dug into his shoulder now. The businessman shook him off and snarled, "How dare you!" He fell suddenly silent when a click sounded in his ear and cold steel pushed against the back of his head.

"I'm no fool," Batts said easily. "When I threaten someone bigger, I ensure the odds are in my favor."

Robinson, frozen, couldn't even nod.

Batts stepped back half a pace, keeping his pistol at the ready. "If you please, Mr. Smythe."

Smythe had, impossibly, grown three shades paler. "Mr. Robinson channels the laundered art to buyers, then launders the income through shell companies and sends it to…" He turned away and bit his fist.

"I deny that," Robinson muttered, carefully so as not to get shot.

"You would," Batts said. "You'd lie to God himself, confident you'd deceive Him. A regular Satan, you are." He moved on. "And the lovely Kate Pollack, still outwardly beautiful after all these years, her beauty concealing the blackest heart of all."

"Don't you dare touch me," she snapped.

"I wouldn't poison myself so. Mr. Smythe, if you please?"

"Say one word," Pollack warned Pal Smythe, "and you're dead."

Batts pressed the gun to the back of Pollack's head. "I would regret nothing."

"Ms. Pollack," Smythe said, head hung in shame, "receives the laundered money. It finances her operation to bring..." He shook his head and squeezed his eyes shut.

"Yes, Mr. Smythe?"

"Women. Poor women. For..." He looked up suddenly. "Please, stop this!"

"What's this, Mr. Smythe? Regret? But why? You've profited so handsomely! Will you not lie to me as they have, as you've lied to yourself these past four years? Let us savor your evil. Deny profiting from their scheme. Deny blackmailing them."

Smythe slipped from the sofa and fell on his knees, keening. The others, screaming obscenities, lunged and, without regard for Batts and his gun, fell upon Smythe, pummeling, kicking, throttling, until he lay dead on the floor. Shaking in anger and fright, they turned on Batts, who encompassed them with a sweep of his weapon.

They froze, a hideous tableau of rage and murder, their victim sprawled at their feet.

"By the by," Batts said easily, "our little party is being video recorded. Won't you smile for the cameras?" He smiled to demonstrate how. When they didn't, he asked, "Sure you don't want some poison cookies?"

In shock, Mr. and Mrs. Phillips shuffled to the love seat and sank into it, clinging to each other. Robinson fell into the recliner and kicked Smyth's body one more time, and why not? Neither man's fate could worsen. Kate Pollack alone remained standing. She crossed her arms over her chest and glared like a general defying hopeless odds, refusing to surrender. "I've done nothing wrong."

Batts shrugged. "Save murder and human trafficking. And selling out your own gender. Do you sleep at night?"

"Like a baby."

Batts took aim at her forehead. "Easier than putting down a dog," he assured her.

"Then do it. You're on candid camera, too."

"Don't be an idiot, Kate," Robinson said. "He owns the cameras. He won't be implicated."

"True, Mr. Robinson." Batts waggled the gun. "So what do we do now, do you suppose?"

Robinson looked ready to commit a second murder. "It's your show, Batts. You tell us."

Batts sighed, pleased. "He can be taught. I want Mr. Smythe's profits. No, moreso."

"We didn't know it was him," Mr. Phillips muttered. "Not until just now."

"Yes," Batts said with syrupy sadness. "Pity you killed him just as you were getting to know him. He was such a kind-hearted blackmailer. The amount you've paid him to date, doubled, in a lump sum."

The gathering stared at Batts as though he'd lost his mind. He shrugged. "My personal contribution to our thirty minutes of evil."

Robinson laughed bitterly. "You could have killed Smythe yourself and taken his place without all this. We'd have never known."

"This is more gratifying. Transfer the money, if you please. To Smythe's account, as usual."

Robinson pulled his cell phone from his trouser pocket and made the arrangements while Batts watched from a distance to prevent a scuffle. By the time it was done, their thirty minutes had long since evaporated, but as the gun was still at the ready, none complained about the overtime.

Payment complete, Robinson pocketed his phone. "Now, I suppose, we go home and pretend this didn't happen?"

"No, Mr. Robinson. I don't think any of you, not even Ms. Pollack, could manage that pretense."

"Then what?" Kate Pollack demanded. If she could have reached him without being shot, she would have strangled him and enjoyed every minute. Batts could tell. He smiled and hoped he looked thoroughly evil.

To be fair, Batts told himself in later years, he regretted Smythe's end. Not his death, but the manner of it. And Robinson and Pollack went far too peacefully, a quick shot to each heart, a moment of surprise, little time for terror. That should have been Smythe's fate, not theirs. *And that*, he admitted to himself, *is on me.*

But the rest worked out fine. Batts felt a moment of elation when Mr. Phillips instinctively caught the empty gun Batts had wiped clean and tossed at him. Left in the lurch, the couple was charged and convicted on three counts of murder. They had protested, Mrs. Phillips particularly. But their connections to the deceased unwound, nobody named Batts could be found—leastwise none matching the description she gave—and neither witnesses nor alleged video footage surfaced. Not even their defense attorney believed them. Mrs. Phillips' ravings waxed hysterical until Mr. Phillips, under relentless interrogation, admitted to occasional assignations with prostitutes at Kate Pollack's many safe houses, of which the murder house was one.

Yes, on the whole it had gone well. Batts rendered the money trail untraceable and afterward didn't dwell on it. He had every intention of donating the whole sum to help victims of human trafficking. It was just, well, it didn't turn out that way. Mere happenstance, really. His cybersecurity career kept him busy, and shortly he met a special woman, married, had a couple of children, grew old, had grandchildren.

Time raced by. He invested some of the take and poured the rest into a comfortable life, and really, could he be blamed for that? In the main, he had no trouble sleeping at night.

Yet on rare occasions, just on the edge of sleep, he'd hear Kate Pollack accuse him of stretching his thirty minutes into a lifetime. She would smile as she said it.

And looked thoroughly evil.

The Boss

"Quinnell MacGabhan, how would you like to die?"

That wasn't a question Quinnell fielded very often, or at all, really, but he had no trouble answering. "Not very much, thank you." He scampered out of reach of the huge, clawed hand swooping down to grab him.

"I mean, by what method. Hold still. You're making this far too difficult."

Quinnell wasn't about to make it easy. A lanky five-foot nine, he had the advantage in maneuverability, even if his charcoal business suit and shiny black oxfords were less than ideal for evading monsters in a frozen wasteland. His opponent, whatever it was, couldn't exactly turn on a dime. The beast towered over him, fifteen feet of carnosaur, or whatever. It stomped around on massive six-toed feet, swiping at Quinnell with the six dagger-clawed fingers of its right hand. Two small fangs protruded from its bottom lip, and its flame-red scales looked more suited to a dragon than a theropod, but Quinnell wouldn't argue classification. Priority one was staying alive.

He scampered over the ice field, slipping and sliding, pursued by the beast. Dodging its grasp, he dove behind a frozen boulder, rolled over the steel-hard ground, and sprang to his feet, shaking from exertion. It lumbered after him. Making a U-turn, he ran straight for it and dove face-first onto the ice. He skidded between its legs, scrambled up, and made for another group of boulders. His muscles burned from exertion.

"You have a choice," it rumbled. Its voice had all the charm of a freight train colliding with a pile of steel girders. "Drowning or being crushed."

The boulders formed a shattered ridge eight feet tall, rimed and spattered with puffs of snow. Quinnell slipped behind and crouched down. Panting, he wondered if could talk the beast into inactivity. He was a lawyer, after all. It was worth a shot. "What *are* you, anyway?"

"Oh, you couldn't pronounce it. Just think of me as a terrifying ice god."

Oddly, Quinnell wasn't terrified, just exhausted and confused. It was hard to be terrified in such a ludicrous situation. How had a finance lawyer from Chicago's northwest suburbs landed here? While no stranger to ice and snow, he'd never seen anything like this. An arctic wasteland? A giant bright red monster? The sky was chartreuse, for God's sake! And that ice covering absolutely everything was electric blue!

"Where am I?"

"Full of questions, aren't you?" The creature zeroed in on his voice and blundered around the frozen rocks, its scaly body contrasting sharply with the scenery. It gazed down on Quinnell with soft, green eyes before making a grab for him. Quinnell vaulted over a chuck of ice and skittered away before the clawed hand could close on him.

"A few answers might be nice!" He puffed the words before jumping a small crevasse that opened at his feet.

"Afraid I don't have any. Not my job to answer questions." The creature pursued, its giant strides closing the distance in moments. The ground shook as its feet struck the ice.

Quinnell reversed course and skidded past the beast before it could nab him. "So what, exactly, *is* your job?"

"Killing you, of course, which would be a lot less unpleasant for you if you held still."

"Don't think so."

The creature made a fist and struck the ground. Cracks split the ice, radiating out from the impact zone. They raced by Quinnell and multiplied, fracturing the landscape in front of him. He skidded to a stop just as the splinters fell away to reveal a deep purple ocean. The unnatural water splashed over everything and froze, covering rocks and ice and Quinnell's fancy suit with purple frosting. Just before he took the plunge, he grabbed a pink rock pinnacle jutting through the ice and torqued his body around. His shoulder screamed as though he'd nearly ripped his arm off.

Doubled over to catch his breath, he glanced up. The beast was advancing more slowly now, sensing its prey was trapped between it and the water. Drown or be crushed, it had said. It looked like this was it. "Why me? I'm just a lawyer!"

"Whine, whine, whine. You chose this destiny, Quinnell MacGabhan."

"Oh, sure, everyone hates lawyers, is that it? What, did you get sued and lose your—well, I don't suppose you ever had a shirt to lose. You're not wearing anything to begin with."

That seemed to puzzle the monster. It stopped, hands on hips, and cocked its head. "What's a lawyer?"

"How do you know my name but not what a lawyer is?"

It straightened its arms and flexed its fingers. Its iridescent claws glittered in the strange light. "I know everyone who chooses to be my victim, but not much else. Knowing things isn't my job."

"That puts us in a rather awkward position, don't you think?" Keep the brute talking, keep the brute talking, keep the brute talking. He glanced around but could see no escape. The ice was shattering, the ocean encroaching. He had no place to run.

"Not at all. I do my job, you do yours, and everything ends as it should."

"With me dead."

"Right." The monster took a step forward but stopped when Quinnell held up a hand.

"Look, I didn't choose anything. I don't even know how I got here. One minute I was reviewing a contract for a client, the next I was here."

With an ironic smile, the creature shook its head. "Took a little break, though, didn't you?"

He couldn't remember much, only that he'd been at his desk, working, and then here he was.

"Uh-huh," the monster said, as though Quinnell had admitted everything.

It started to move, but once more Quinnell stopped it with a gesture. Brains didn't seem to be its forte. It hadn't noticed the ice around its feet was now riddled with hairline cracks from the stress of its weight.

"What?" it asked irritably.

"So, you basically wait around here to kill people?"

"You got it."

"That's your whole life?"

"Pretty much."

"Doesn't that bother you?"

"No, it makes me very happy." The creature smiled happily.

"Killing people." Quinnell gave his best skeptical look, like he was grilling a lying witness. Not that he had any trial experience. He wasn't that kind of lawyer. But some of his friends were.

"Look—" Ice splintered around the creature's massive feet. It tottered a bit, arms thrown wide for balance. "I don't make the rules, okay? I just do my job. You meet the boss monster, he tries to kill you. That's how it works."

"Boss monster?"

It tapped its chest proudly. "Boss monster. Terrifying ice god at the end of level six."

Quinnell blinked and nearly let the monster make a move. He threw up his hands just in time.

With a huge sigh, it set its fists back on its hips.

"Are you saying this is a video game?"

"A what?" Little explosions went off all around its feet. It nearly toppled. Shattered blocks fell into the ocean with tremendous splashes. The beast was left standing on a floating chunk of ice that rocked haphazardly on the frothy purple ocean.

"A video game!" Quinnell wasn't faring much better. The land around him was disintegrating, too, leaving him but a few square feet to stand.

"Don't know what that is. All I know is, you chose to spend time in my world, so here you are, waiting to die by my hand."

He supposed he must have fallen asleep on the contract and was now immersed in a dream. A very realistic, if strange, dream. "What if I kill you instead?"

The creature laughed. "You can't." The ice beneath it rocked from side to side. It looked down and frowned just as the last block popped out from under it. With a great splash that soaked everything in horrid purple water, the boss monster plunged into the sea, arms flailing. Just before its head vanished beneath the waves, it called, "I always come back!"

Quinnell watched bubbles break the surface. At least that was over. Maybe now he could wake up and find himself comfortably ensconced in his office, pages and pages of legalese spread before him, all soothing and totally, totally normal.

While he waited for that blessed moment to come, he pondered the source of the dream. He didn't play video games. Absolute waste of time. He'd spent years trying to get his son to see that, all the while fending off the kid's attempts to suck him into one outlandish game after another.

"Beg your pardon," a new voice said behind him.

Had he succumbed to the pressure? Had he indeed taken a break to play some idiotic...

"Ahem!"

Turning, Quinnell found himself in an orange and pink desert edged with rainbow sherbet sand dunes and marshmallow clouds drifting through a milk chocolate sky. Seated halfway up a dune, a rat-like creature studied him with glowing mauve eyes.

"What's this, now?" Quinnell asked nobody.

"Next level," the rat said.

"I'm not playing any further. I'm waking up now."

The rat cocked its head. "What do you mean, waking up?"

"I'm turning the game off."

"Don't know about any game," his new adversary remarked, "but you're stuck with me, pal. So."

It smiled an ugly, toothy smile.

"Quinnell MacGabhan, how would you like to die?"

Down by Two

The rust-red stone tumbled down the slope in slow motion and came to rest in the arms of a creosote bush. "Ten points," Clara announced, pumping her fists in the air.

"Eight," Piotr objected. "Wasn't dead center." When she raised an eyebrow, he added, "But a good kick." The sky had darkened to indigo. He adjusted his clear bubble helmet and tugged at his wafer-thin coveralls. "Better call it there."

"When you're ahead by two? Figures."

"Temperature's dropping, Commander."

He loved his excuses. "We should have been genetically modified, like them." Clara waved at the clumps of gray-green-brown clinging like fungus to the rusty soil. "Nothing's gone right, and here we are, me two points down and the game's been called."

They began the long trudge up the slope to base, the only warm, fully oxygenated spot on Mars. "They'll get us back," Piotr said with faux confidence.

Rock crunched under Clara's boots. The recirculated air inside her suit smelled of rubber. What she wouldn't give to smell roses or lilacs again. "Nobody's interested. Terraforming didn't happen with a snap of the fingers, so it's been dumped in the trash, like everything else humans do. And us with it."

Darkness pulled its blanket over the eastern sky. A few stars peeked through. Piotr said nothing.

"Table tennis," Clara suggested. "A bag of those awful plastic cookies to the winner."

Piotr kicked a rock to the side. "You'll lose," he predicted. "By two."

The End of Everything

Their feet crunched through the ash. The sound transported Laszlo back to autumn leaves thick on the ground, red, orange, and gold embers of a burned-out summer, only this stuff had fallen black and cold from crumbling limbs, and anyway, it was only spring.

They came prepared, of course. They wore hats, goggles, gloves, boots. Their faces were wrapped, their nostrils and mouths shielded behind breathing filters. They felt neither the sun on their cheeks nor the wind in their hair. Laszlo kicked the ash. Motes looped through the air and fluttered feather-soft back to Earth.

"Don't do that, Laz. Breath this stuff and you're dead in half an hour."

Laszlo wished his friend Whistler wouldn't be so dramatic. Spectacle may have served him well on the basketball court as they led their college to three championships, but that streak ended eight years ago. Then, the world seemingly had half a chance of spinning on for a few more centuries. He wondered if anyone watching them walk the deserted road now would see them as they once were: Whistler the wisecracking team captain, Laszlo the ebony scholar, a pair of giants, a matched set of contradictions. But nobody watched. Treading the black crust of a dying world, they were but two of the survivors, not giants, not legends, not anything at all.

He tapped Whistler's breathing filter. "That's what these are for."

"These? The dust is so fine, it slips right through the filter. It clogs your alveoli so oxygen can't get into your blood. Bam. Dead."

Black dust swirled about their feet. You couldn't escape it or the poison within. All that was green and much that wasn't had succumbed to the toxin. Carried on the wind, the ash coated streets, cars, houses, everything. Whether you breathed it, swallowed it, or touched it, sooner or later it would pollute you, consume you from the inside. You might asphyxiate or bleed or become a mass of tumors. Time wasn't on your side.

"No point dwelling on it," Laszlo said.

Houses lined the road, nice ones, temples to consumption now reduced to soot-coated husks, their stored-up treasures relics before which none would ever again bow. A few blocks west, a once-busy intersection hosted a dilapidated gas station, a silent fast food drive-through, and the men's destination, a grocery store still stocked with canned goods and desiccated meats and vegetables. Little seemed to rot anymore. Whistler thought microorganisms must have been wiped out by the poison, too.

Laszlo didn't know about that. Their lives depended on that unseen world, didn't they? But he wouldn't obsess over that, either. Survival alone occupied him. He figured the store's remaining canned goods might get them through the coming year.

"I'm not dwelling on anything," Whistler said. "I'm just saying—"

"You're grandstanding like you always do."

"I'm just saying—"

"There's no audience, W! Nobody's cheering for you, nobody's in awe of you. It's just you and me and all this *dust*!" Laszlo kicked the black again. It swirled up three feet and spun away on the breeze.

They walked on to the grocery store. Laszlo found himself thinking back anyway, back to his girlfriend Fawn, back to their joy upon learning they had a baby girl on the way. But like all happiness, that had blown away on the dust. Fawn had miscarried and bled to death.

"It was in the water, you know," Whistler said. "In the lakes and rivers, even in the rain. Then it was in the soil, and the plants took it up. No more trees. No more flowers. No more food."

Laszlo didn't answer.

"That's how it happened."

"We'd better take two carts. We need as much water as we can haul."

They crunched across the grocery store parking lot. "It's in the bottled water, too. They found it there, in the end. Everyone thought *that* was safe, only it wasn't. Well, not everyone. The company knew, forty-eight years ago. When the truth came out, they developed a replacement chemical, and that was even worse, and when that was banned, they developed another replacement, and that was worse still."

Outside the door, a line of neatly mated carts awaited customers who would never come. Laszlo yanked the two end carts from the line and pushed them through the door. "Just shut up, okay? What about the future? Isn't that more important?" They'd had this argument before in numerous forms. God willing, they would live long enough to have it another thousand times. He undocked the two carts and gave one to Whistler.

"I'm not the one kicking up dust," Whistler objected.

"Let's just get what we—"

A crash echoed through the store.

Frozen, Laszlo and Whistler could barely breathe. Somewhere among the shelves, feet pounded the floor.

Whistler motioned. Abandoning their carts, they crept along the front of the store between the aisles and the silent checkout lines. At each aisle they paused and peered around the corner before passing it by. When they reached the third aisle from the end, they heard plastic rattling. There Laszlo found a small figure with its back to them tearing open a candy bag. Astonished, he slowly approached with Whistler right behind.

The child turned, startled. A girl of nine with matted hair strung about her shoulders, she stared wide-eyed at them, the open candy bag clutched in both hands.

Laszlo stopped so as not to frighten her further.

"Mommy's hungry," the girl said, her voice quavering.

Whistler came to his side. "It's okay. We won't hurt you. Where is your mommy?"

The girl pointed behind her. "At home. Not far." She wasn't wearing any protection, just a grimy pair of faded jeans and a long sleeve blouse with an unzipped red jacket thrown over. Flecks of black dust clung to the fabric. She had no gloves, no facial covering, no breathing filter.

"What's your name?" Whistler asked.

"Evanthe."

"I'm Whistler. This is Laszlo."

Evanthe laughed in spite of her fear.

"Really, those are our names. We're getting food, too. We could take some to your mommy."

"Okay," Evanthe said.

Laszlo didn't know about that. With four people consuming them, the store's supplies would run out nearly twice as fast, even if one mouth was still small. He tapped Whistler's shoulder and whispered his objection.

"We can't just leave her here," Whistler said.

"How long's she going to last? She's not wearing protection. Her mother's probably already dying, or she'd be here herself."

"But Laz—"

"It's the end of everything, W. It's every man for himself."

Whistler looked back at Evanthe who was still clutching the bag, still staring at them with those dark, wide eyes. "Every man for himself destroyed us. You said we should think about the future. Well, this is the future." He nodded toward the girl.

Laszlo met Evanthe's gaze. He couldn't see any future there, only death. But then she blinked, and time rewound. Laszlo found himself staring into another pair of eyes, eyes he had only ever imagined. His daughter's eyes.

"Laz?" Whistler asked.

It might have been the dust, the poison, the loss, the stress. He didn't know. Whatever it was, past, present, and future folded together in the dark of Evanthe's pupils. Time became irrelevant. It was always the end of everything. It always had been, always would be. Today, tomorrow, a year, a decade, a century—whenever death came, it would come, unstoppable. All he had, all any of them had, was now.

"Sure," he said. He held out his hand. "Come on, Evanthe. Let's do some shopping."

Sherlock Holmes and the Case of the Drive-Thru Cheeseburger

"Americans," Sherlock Holmes said in his offhand manner, "have perfected the art of the inedible." He dropped his uneaten cheeseburger into his lap, where the paper wrapper caught it. "Yet they criticize us for lack of culinary flair."

En route to the scene of a curious theft in Buntingford that had baffled Scotland Yard, we paused at an American franchise, a Burger Bazaar drive-through on the outskirts of Thundridge on the River Rib. I was driving. Holmes had become notorious as Britain's most reckless driver, and his license had been suspended for the seventh time in three years. Though luncheon had passed—indeed, it was nearly afternoon tea—he showed no interest in dining. I, however, was famished, and since I had charge of the steering wheel, he was forced to acquiesce to the demands of my rumbling stomach.

"How can you eat that, Watson?" he continued. "As usual, you see but do not observe."

Having parked and unwrapped my food, I had no interest in deduction. "I'm starving to death," I explained. "My focus is on consuming the product, not analyzing its potential role as criminal evidence."

"Precisely my point."

"Really, Holmes. It's quite impossible that anyone was coshed to death with this cheeseburger."

Holmes smiled a thin smile. "There are crimes apart from murder, Watson, some of which might involve..." He picked up and scrutinized his own lunch. "Beef products." He dropped it again. "Consider this bun. What do you note?"

"That it consists of cheap bread."

I lifted my sandwich, but he put a hand to my arm to stop me. "Indeed. Unusually thin for a hamburger bun, with a glossy crust and a consistency that bespeaks substantial air pockets. This bun is more oxygen than wheat. It was baked in a factory intent upon excessive minimization of expense. As you're aware, I've made an extensive study of baked goods. This bun came from the Tittynope Grain Factory in Buntingford."

"The very town to which we've been summoned? But Holmes, that case involves the theft of a dozen wedding gowns."

"Correct, Watson. Recall the peculiar twist that renders the case a singularly perplexing puzzle: what the thief left in place of the gowns."

"A dozen purple bikini bottoms," I confirmed. "But what does that have to do with buns?" No sooner had the words escaped my lips than I realized I'd been tricked. "Hamburger buns," I irritably amended.

Feigning innocence, Holmes broke off a smidgeon of meat and popped it in his mouth. "Also note the high salt content, evident from the grotesque flavor. The quantity of grease congealed on the wrapper attests to the inferior quality of the meat. And consider the miniscule application of condiments and toppings: a dab of mayonnaise, a partially wilted lettuce leaf, a thin slice of underripe tomato. This is a criminally cheap sandwich, Watson, of such low estate as to be all but inedible."

I concluded Holmes was joking, his jest in as bad taste as the cheeseburger itself. Did he mean to ruin my appetite? Angry, I moved to shove the sandwich into my mouth to spite him, but he caught my arm again. "Holmes!" I blustered. "What in the name of God is this about?"

"You may not want to eat that, Watson. Have you not noticed? Your sandwich is rather unlike mine."

I examined my cheeseburger and found he was right. The bun was generously topped with sesame seeds. Toppings and condiments overflowed from beneath. Nor was there any trace of grease on my wrapper. Whereas his sandwich was substandard in nearly every detail, mine presented at least the appearance of a hearty meal. "I don't understand," I admitted. "Did we not order the same thing?"

"We did, Watson. Clearly, that sandwich was intended for me, not you."

"How do you deduce that?"

"Elementary. You are but a doctor of good repute and a writer of cheap detective tales. I am Sherlock Holmes. They likely recognized me from my Facebook photo."

Before I could react, Holmes gently relieved me of the cheeseburger and passed me his instead. The import of his words stunned me. I felt like a fool. The cheeseburger was poisoned! "Thank you, Holmes," I blubbered. "Thank you. I'm most grateful."

"Now eat," he said, "and drive. We must arrive in Buntingford with all due haste."

I did as instructed, barely tasting the meal although deriving some modicum of energy from it. Only when finished did I realize Holmes was eating, too.

"Homes!" I blurted. "The poison!"

"Poison, Watson? What poison?"

"But you said..."

Finished, Holmes daintily wiped his fingers with his napkin. "I said you had received the wrong sandwich, Watson. But as usual, your conclusions were wrong in nearly every respect."

The Ghost in the Stacks

The library staff tried everything: denying and ignoring, psychiatrists and parapsychologists, ghost hunters and debunkers. Nothing worked. Oblivious, mocking even, the apparition prowled the stacks with impunity. It browsed the books and walked clean through startled patrons without once begging pardon. Security cameras revealed no sign of its wispy presence. Microphones proved deaf to its feathery footfalls and the rustle of pages turned by its translucent hands. Only people could see or hear the uninvited guest, or rather, certain people. Book people. Serious book people.

Most of the staff saw it, be they young or old, woman or man, black or white or anything in between. A security guard and sometime writer hired to track the apparition after hours watched night after night as it sampled the collected literature. As for others, computer users seldom noticed it, but books-by-the-dozen patrons did, and one in particular: Margot Beach, a high school sophomore of coal black skin and generous smile, a devourer of the written word, who that Saturday afternoon talked with the ghost.

She mentioned it to the library's oldest staffer, reference librarian Joshua Crane, not quite in passing. Crane stopped her with a gape. "It *spoke* to you?"

"Uh-huh," Margot swelled with pride. "And listened!"

"Listened! You mean you *conversed*?"

"Uh-huh!"

He motioned her impatiently to a chair. "What did it say? What did you say? Who is it and why is it here?"

Margo giggled under the barrage. "He's not an it, he's a he."

Crane's eyes sparkled as though he'd discovered a brilliant new author. He leaned forward and asked in confidence, "Come on, Margot, tell all!"

"I asked what he was reading. He said Melville and smiled and pushed up his glasses and—"

"Glasses!"

"Uh-huh. Then he asked my name. When I told him, he said it was his favorite. He asked what *I* was reading, and I said, 'Everything!' and he laughed and said 'That's *right*!' He gave me a book, and poof!" Her fingers spread wide. "He was gone."

Crane scratched his cheek. "You're teasing old Joshua, yes?"

Margo laughed. "Swear to God!"

"What book did he give you?"

She held it up. "*The Scarlet Letter.*"

Crane took it and stroked the cover. It smelled of deep time and felt like dragon skin. He handed it back. "What do you make of him?"

Margo shrugged, "He likes to read." And away she bounded to do likewise.

Of course, Crane couldn't keep quiet. By closing the whole staff knew the whole story, which someone leaked to the local paper, which sent a reporter in search of Margot Beach, whose father refused to grant an interview with his daughter, who was back on a quest for more books the moment the library opened on Sunday.

The library staff had a plan by then, with Joshua Crane in a starring role.

"Now Margot," he whispered, "When you see the ghost, ask his name. Ask why he picked our library. Ask if he plans to stay."

"Sure, he's staying."

"How do you know?"

"The books are here!"

Crane thought it a good reason to stay, but who knew what might be in the mind of a ghost? "Just ask," he said. "We want to be sure."

And off she went in pursuit of her quarry. The whole staff itched to follow, to spy, to eavesdrop, but they feared scaring off the specter. So they waited, feigning immersion in their work, gnawing their nails in anticipation.

Margot had all the time in the world and all the books in the library. She meandered from Dewey Decimal section to Dewey Decimal section, pulled out volumes, sampled pages, book after book, shelf after shelf, occasionally adding to the growing stack of history, science, fantasy, mystery, biography in her arms until she had a pile nearly too tall to juggle.

"You remind me of someone," the ghost said behind her.

She turned. His kindly smile was directed at the book in his shimmering hands. "Of you?" she asked.

"You win the giant stuffed bear," he proclaimed. "A regular sharpshooter, you are."

"How many books can *you* carry?"

"Hundreds," the ghost replied. "Thousands. Millions! Oh, but not in my hands. Hands are small. Up here." He tapped his temple. "I gorge myself, breakfast, lunch, and dinner. Digested words fuel this engine."

The image intrigued her. "You remember them all?"

"Didn't used to. The old file clerk wasn't always the most efficient of secretaries. But death agrees with him, it seems." He shelved one volume and withdrew another. "Now I eat whatever I want and never get full or fat." He glanced at her sheepishly. "You don't mind if I mix my metaphors, do you?"

Margot shook her head. "I think it's fun."

The ghost grinned and went back to his book.

"If you're dead…" Margot stopped, worried it might be indelicate to start that way.

"Very much so," he said gently, "and happy to be. I loved living, sure. I ran twenty times around the equator most days, whooping and hollering the whole way. But death is so much *bigger* than life. Far more space to run!" He winked at her. "Your question?"

"Why aren't you in heaven?"

"Why, Margot," he gasped. "How can you ask that? You, of all people?" He pushed up his glasses and nestled a book on her stack.

"Right," she agreed. "Dumb question."

"Didn't your math teacher say there are no dumb questions?"

"Uh-huh."

"Idiot."

Ghost and young lady laughed long and long.

Their conversation ran several times around the library, through books and writing and life in general, and by the time it was done and the closing announcement spilled from the speakers, Margot Beach thought she'd learned enough for three lifetimes, although probably she wouldn't remember a quarter of it. Only then did she recall Joshua Crane's questions and ask them.

They seemed to irritate the ghost. He slapped his current book shut, stuffed it back in place, and snagged something new. "Why don't they ask for themselves?"

"I think 'cause you only talk to me."

"No, that's not it." But he wouldn't say what it was, and Margot didn't care to press.

"You're here for the books," she asked, "Right?"

"Nope. Any library would do for that. But this one harbors a pearl of great price. That's why I stay." He glanced at her significantly.

Margot blushed. She knew her name's meaning. "I'll leave for college in a few years."

"One with a library, I'm sure."

"You'll follow?"

"I'm a stalker, yes, but I'm not uncivil. I only go where I'm invited. Then, I lurk in the shadows, watching, whispering, seldom seen but often heard. And what invites me? Imagination. Stories. Lovers of words." The ghost looked to the ceiling and sighed. "Library's closing. You'd best be on your way."

"I guess," Margot said. "But who *are* you?"

"An honorary uncle," she explained.

"Uncle?" Joshua Crane walked Margot to the door where her father stood waiting, eyeing her stack of books with amusement and dismay.

"Uh-huh. Uncle Ray."

Crane's fingers brushed his lips. "Ray? Hmm. He mention a last name?"

"He didn't have to." Margot offloaded half her stack into her father's arms and waddled with him to his car.

Not Quite a Ghost Story

One moment the curving road was dry, the chill air clear, then slate clouds scudded through the pass so low Kara might reach up and grab a fistful of mountain mist. As she started down the other side, a sheet of rippling white engulfed her. On her right, the mountainside dropped away into a deep valley, but she couldn't see the edge, the guardrail, not even the asphalt. The snow stole the whole world away.

She braked, fearful of a skid that might spin her into oblivion. From the back seat, Kara's dog whined and thrust his muzzle into her ear. She pushed him back. "Stop it, Knave!"

Knave whined again and pressed his nose to the window. An American Leopard Hound, his brindle coat glowed softly in the diffuse light. He was only two years old, a rescue Kara had adopted. He'd earned his name his first day in her apartment by stealing a bologna sandwich from the kitchen table.

"I know, I know." Kara's fingers wrapped tight about the wheel. She rode the brake to counter the acceleration on the downhill run. "I can't see a thing, either. Maybe I should stop." But where? She couldn't find the shoulder. What if she stopped in the middle of the road and another driver rammed her from behind? Traffic had been light, but a few vehicles were about. Watching for fleeting glimpses of lane markings, she crept onward, sometimes finding herself half in the left lane, sometimes bumping off the right shoulder and getting a too-close glimpse of a rock cliff towering overhead. The snow blew across her bow in rippling streamers.

Knave's face pushed by hers, and he yipped in alarm as a dark shape materialized before them. Breath stuck in her throat, Kara hit the brakes and slid to a stop. She heard nothing, felt nothing, but something was now draped across the hood, dark, indistinguishable.

Oh my God, Kara thought. *I've killed something. Or someone.*

Jumping into the front seat, Knave barked and whined. Kara didn't know what to do. What had she hit? Should she back up? Get out and investigate? She set a trembling hand on Knave's back, seeking comfort in his presence. He barked again, tentatively, apparently having no clear advice.

The figure rose and took on the semblance of a man. Kara pushed back in her seat.

Shaking himself, the apparition rounded the hood and came to her window, tall, stuffed into a parka, his bearded face surrounded by the thick hood. His skin appeared ashen against the swirling snow. She couldn't tell his age. He stood there, looking at her, neither smiling nor frowning, happy nor angry, ghost-pale, a granite statue save that he had moved.

Kara stared back, afraid.

He gently rapped on the window with his black-gloved left hand while raising his right to display a gas can. He mouthed words Kara couldn't quite hear.

She pressed the button to lower the window, stopping before the gap grew wide enough for a hand to reach through. "Are you okay?" she asked.

"Fine," he said. "Could you give me a ride? I ran out of gas."

Horror stories flitted through her mind. Thieves. Rapists. Serial killers. But how could she leave someone stranded in this weather?

Knave cocked his head and, strangely, didn't bark. He normally didn't take to strangers, so Kara took his reticence as a sign that the interloper was safe. She trusted her dog, at least where food wasn't involved. Knave was usually right about people.

She pressed a button, and the locks thunked open. "Get in back. My dog's riding shotgun."

The man slid in and carefully set the gas can on the floor. Once the cold, wind, and snow had been shut out, he pushed back his hood. Kara looked in the rear-view mirror. The warmth of the car didn't improve his pallor, but he looked young, probably about her own age. He had a full head of dark hair and smoky eyes. The effect unsettled her. "You're not a ghost, are you?" She forced a laugh.

He gave her a thin smile, cooler than humor, warmer than the snow. "The next exit should be two miles up. There's a gas station there. What's your name?"

She put the car in gear and inched forward. "Kara. What's yours?"

"You're pretty, Kara."

The reflection of his eyes in the mirror, as colorless as the storm, met hers. Why had he said *that*? She didn't find her own reflection anything special: face a bit too round, dishwater blonde hair a bit too straight. She really should lose some weight, too. Maybe reality looked different to a ghost? Turning her attention back to the road, she drove on without comment.

She heard him settle into the seat. "Why are you out here on a day like this?" he asked.

None of your business, she thought. "Family business," she said. She glanced at Knave, who remained uncharacteristically quiet. The dog watched the interloper with keen eyes but seemed not the least concerned by his presence. "What about you?" Kara suddenly realized she hadn't seen his car, not even in vaguest outline. How had he gotten there on the road, holding a gas can, with no car? Maybe he really was a ghost. Maybe he'd been sent by…

Don't be ridiculous, she scolded herself.

"Making deliveries." He slowly extended a hand to Knave. "Good boy," he said gently. "Good dog."

Knave stretched his nose to the proffered hand, sniffed, licked.
"I guess he likes me."

The road twisted left, rose, bent right, fell. Kara tracked along it, still unable to see more than occasional flashes of lines. The snow refused to yield, but at least it hadn't stuck much to the road. Occasionally it granted her a glimpse of the demarcation between safety and danger.

The stranger scratched Knave behind the ears. "You like traveling, don't you, Knave?"

Knave panted acknowledgement.

Stunned, Kara checked her passenger in the mirror again. "How do you know his name? Do I know you?"

He lifted one of the tags hanging from Knave's collar. "It says so here." He dropped it and scratched Knave behind the ears again. "Honest, I'm no ghost. I'm just a delivery driver."

Kara peered into the whiteout. A hint of green flickered in the distance, maybe a sign announcing the next exit. "You never said your name."

"John Smith." When she neither answered nor looked back, he added, "That's why I didn't say it. You wouldn't have believed me. But I swear, that's my name."

"What are you delivering in this blizzard, Mr. Smith?" The sign passed by, vaguely green, all but impossible to read.

"Nothing, until I get some gas and get back to my van."

"I didn't see a van."

"It's mostly white."

If he was a ghost, he had an explanation for every odd thing. Probably he wasn't, then, which disappointed her a little. She could welcome a ghost sent by her brother Dan into this storm with words of assurance and comfort. But Dan was stone cold dead at age fifty-three, victim of a brain tumor. His funeral would be tomorrow in Morristown.

The road took a spin to the left. Kara almost missed it, almost took out the guardrail. The drop-off must be on her side of the road again. Shaking from adrenaline, she deflected the danger with a question. "What do you deliver when you have gas?"

"Flowers."

"Flowers?"

"Flowers. Gift flowers, wedding flowers, funeral flowers. It's a job." She heard the shrug in his voice. "Morristown's my next stop, if I ever get there."

"Morristown!" Kara pulled over and threw the gear into park. She turned on the interloper. Knave shoved his face into hers and licked her cheek. John Smith waited, expressionless, almost not breathing. She wanted him out of the car but only found one word. "Morristown!"

"Morristown," he acknowledged. "Some—"

"Funeral home," they said simultaneously.

Knave licked Kara's face again and gave John Smith a pleading look. John took pity on the creature and provided another head scratch. "There's the exit," he said helplessly.

Beside the car, a blue sign peeked through the snow, pointing the way to a gas station. Kara put the car in motion and picked her way down the ramp.

"Who's funeral?" John asked.

"My brother's."

"I'm sorry."

A snow-splattered stop sign marked the end of the ramp. Beside it, another blue gas sign pointed right. Kara turned. "How does a professional driver run out of gas?" She bit her lip. She hadn't meant it to sound so mean. Or maybe she did. Maybe it was payback for him going where she was going.

"Stupidity. Paying more attention to the storm than the gauge."

She pulled into the station and stopped by a pump.

"Thanks," he said. He picked up his gas can and slid out.

She about let him close the door without response, until Knave gave her a head butt. The dog's eyes seemed to say, "It's not John's fault. It was just the storm, just a coincidence, just a quirk of fate. In fact, he was lucky we came along."

"Wait," she said. "How will you get back?"

"Haven't figured that out yet."

"I can take you."

"You've done enough already. Driving in that storm--"

"It's okay. I don't mind."

John leaned his ashen face into the car. "You sure?"

Kara nodded.

"Well. Thank you." He laughed for the first time since they'd met. "Are you sure *you're* not a ghost?"

"Me?"

"You thought I was. You thought your brother sent me. Didn't you?"

Kara didn't dare answer that. Knave barked on her behalf. *Traitor*, she silently scolded.

"Maybe it was the other way 'round. Maybe he sent you to rescue me."

John closed the door, swiped his credit card, filled his container.

While Kara waited, Knave slupped her face once more. She pushed him away. "Oh, stop it." But Knave didn't want to stop, and she had to push him away again. "I know what you're thinking," she accused. "You're wrong. We won't see him again after today. You'll see."

But even she wasn't so sure. Knave, after all, was usually right about people.

Goldenrod is Here

Mark remembered two things about that night, one being the fog creeping up the slope from the distant riverbank, slinking like a gray cat among the trees, slithering down the narrow streets, creeping around houses with their curtain eyelids drawn in slumber. The other was his cell phone, guzzling electrons on the faux Jacobean nightstand while warbling the quiet tune that meant Stacey was calling. The music woke him, but oddly he remembered the silence of the fog preceding it.

He reached, grabbed, and answered, eyes clamped stubbornly shut. "Where are you?" His other hand finger-walked across the bed and grabbed a fistful of linen where Stacey ought to have been. "What time is it?" He blinked himself to awareness, stood, stumbled to the window, yanked open the curtains. The fog rolled lazily by.

"Goldenrod is here," Stacey's static-streaked voice told him.

"Who?"

"Goldenrod. Our cat."

The fog tried to worm its way through the window frame. Cold damp licked Mark's fingers. He jerked his hand back and drew the curtains in haste. "We don't have a cat. Where are you?" Sitting on the bed, he tried to think. What time was it?

The phone ought to know, but its face was coal-black, and the crackling voice had fallen still. He set the device on the nightstand and settled back into bed. "Where are you?" he repeated.

"I'm here, Mark. I'm here." Stacy set a light hand on his shoulder and jostled him. "Wake up. You'll be late for work."

Work. Right. Mark sat, blinked at the sunlight filtering through the curtains, blinked at his phone. He switched to past tense. "Where were you?"

"When?" She rolled out of the sheets and sat beside him, warm, comfortable, her arm about his waist. She'd always been that. Warm. Comfortable. She'd been more, too, once upon a time, but as their relationship mellowed, the magic slipped away. That wasn't bad. It just was.

"Last night," he said. "When you called."

"Bathroom, I suppose. You probably heard the water running."

He scooped up the phone and checked it. The call log showed her number at three-oh-three. Mark shoved it under her nose. "So what's this?"

Stacy cocked her head. "Somebody spoofed my number? Weird. Funny time for a robocall, too."

What was easier to believe? That he was going nuts, or that she was lying? "I'm calling in sick," he decided, and she watched, bemused, while he did.

Stacey dressed extra nice—best blue dress, best white heels, best string of artificial pearls—but not for Mark. "District manager's coming today," she said over toast and coffee. "He probably won't even set foot in our area, but we all have to be ready. Just in case."

Wisps of thought drifted aimlessly through Mark's brain like fog, like cats yowling in the night. Thoughts about fog and cats and his wife's presence and absence and presence while phones sounded in the dark. Already the facts, if facts they were, were burning off in the morning sun, leaving a clear view of a land he had known for twenty-three years. A sound marriage. Two daughters now in college, a good home in a good suburb, a neatly trimmed lawn bordered with mostly weed-free flowerbeds. Good jobs, acceptable bank accounts and retirement plans, a faithful old dog buried last year, and absolutely no cats. They had fallen in love young, had dreamed of a magic life, had slipped into okayness. They had grown old enough to find a measure of wisdom but remained young enough that old age seemed a thousand years off. Neither bored with nor tired of each other, Mark and Stacey eased down time's forest road, hand in hand because it was right and natural, and anyway neither could think of anything better to do. Magic no, but they were content in the sameness of every daybreak and nightfall.

That's how it had been. That's how it remained. Ergo, he must have dreamed strange dreams, because mysteries just didn't happen in this house. Where would Stacey be in the middle of the night but sleeping at his side or, as she'd said, in the bathroom?

She left for work. He read the online news until his eyes glazed over. Ten thirty came and went, and with it the mail carrier, a young black woman with a quick step, a wireless gadget in her ear, and a running conversation with a friend spilling from her lips all over the otherwise quiet neighborhood. Mark watched her pass down the street before retrieving the day's credit card offers from the curbside mailbox. Leafing through them on the way back, he nearly stepped on an orange cat that had materialized from the ether and curled up on his doormat. It blinked at him with sleepy eyes and yawned a fierce-toothed tiger yawn.

A bit of that early morning fog drifted through Mark's head.

The cat didn't budge, nor was it wearing a collar.

"Scat," Mark commanded. "Git. Shoo."

The cat gazed across the yard to a robin poking in the grass but showed no inclination to hunt.

"Go on." Mark waved vigorously to no avail. "Fine. Stay there. I'm not feeding you." He turned the knob, stepped quickly over the animal, and definitively closed the door.

Before he could take another step, something purred and rubbed against his leg. The orange cat, looking hopeful.

"No!" Mark yanked the door open and nudged the cat out with his shoe. Alone again, he retreated to the kitchen for a caffeine boost, but there before the dishwasher was the cat, sitting with perfect cat posture, tail wrapped elegantly about its feet, its glare now decidedly accusing.

The rest of the morning was a blur, chasing the cat, carting the cat, exteriorizing the cat time after time after time only to have it show up again in the damnedest places, from the top of the bookcase in the study to behind the potted gardenia in the living room, from the bathroom sink to snuggled beneath the guest bed comforter.

Finally, about noon and a half, Mark gave up, flopped on the sofa, and hid his face in his arm. "I'm going to sleep," he told nobody, "and when I wake this nightmare will be over!"

Naturally, he didn't sleep. But the cat did. It leaped onto the far arm of the sofa, slunk step by silent step along the back, and oozed onto his chest, where it curled into a warm, purring mass of golden fur.

"I should strangle you," he told it. "Nine times. Ten, for good measure. Maybe eleven, just to be sure you can't come back."

The cat might have had nine hundred lives, for all the threat concerned it.

His cell phone was playing Stacey's tune again, muffled deep within his pocket. So much for sleep. He dug it out without opening his eyes. "What's up?" he asked.

"Goldenrod is here," she said.

"Who?"

"Goldenrod. Our cat."

"We don't have a cat." Or at least they hadn't. Had they? Something niggled at him. No, not a something, a nothing, an absence, a something missing. He sat and ran a hand through his hair. "What time is it?" He swung his legs off the sofa and stood. Nothing purred at his feet or rubbed against his legs. Nothing had been sleeping on his chest. He felt a bit cold, a bit hollow, and more than a little hungry.

"I must've missed lunch," he told Stacey. She wasn't there anymore. He looked at his phone and found its face coal-black, so he shoved it back into his pocket and flopped on the sofa again. A few deep breaths later, she spoke, but not from the phone, not with respect to missing a meal.

"Who's this?" she asked.

Something purred on Mark's chest.

He opened his eyes and found Stacey scratching the cat behind the ears.

"This?" He thought for a moment. "This is Goldenrod."

They had to buy stuff they'd never bought before: cat food and dishes, litter boxes and litter. One litter box per cat plus one, Mark discovered online. Who'd have thought it wouldn't be just one? They put word around that an orange cat had been found. They took Goldenrod to the vet and learned the animal was a she in perfect health, minus microchip and kitten-making equipment. Somebody must have owned her very recently, but nobody came forward to claim her, and she displayed no inclination to leave. Stacey readily fell in love with the critter.

Yet all was not bliss. The comfortable sameness of life had been disrupted by fog, phones, and cats. Mark couldn't fathom any of it, especially not Goldenrod's feats of teleportation. He could just about put the phone's misbehavior down to dreams, except Goldenrod had been in them. Conversely, Goldenrod's defiance of physics occurred while Mark was wide awake. It seemed exactly backwards.

So he turned to the tools of science, or as much science as he knew. He observed, noted, and charted Goldenrod's movements in an attempt to pull back the veil. He spied upon his cell phone as he fell asleep each night, waiting for it to ring, waiting for Stacey to call and announce Goldenrod's whereabouts. He watched her, too, although he felt like a spy as he secretly logged her comings and goings. He spontaneously woke in the middle of most nights, dreading her absence. She was always there.

But was he all there? That was an open question. These mysteries drove him to the brink of sleep-deprived madness made madder by their sudden absence. No calls. No teleporting cats. No missing wives. Just the same predictable life as always, save his mania and Goldenrod.

Stacey couldn't help but notice he wasn't quite right. "Maybe we should take some time off," she gently suggested one evening. "Go somewhere. You've always wanted to see Yosemite."

He had, but he couldn't, not with experiments in progress. They were at the dinner table finishing their store-bought apple pie with an excuse fortuitously purring in his lap. "We have nobody to watch Goldenrod," he objected.

"We can board her at the vet's, Mark. Come on, let's do this."

Goldenrod stopped purring and looked up. Mark knew what she was saying: *Don't you dare leave me in that awful place!*

But his wife wouldn't be dissuaded, so eventually they put in for vacation, reserved a kitty cage, got their tickets, and by the time they reached the hotel, Mark had forgotten all about his amateur science project.

A bank of cloud floated over the tops of the mountains and crept down the slopes, enveloping pines and fields, wildlife and visitors, parking lots and hotels. Wrapped in its cool embrace, the land shivered and awaited the morning sun. But it was only a little after three, and Mark's phone was playing Stacey's tune. He answered automatically without opening his eyes. "Where are you?" He felt for her in the night, but she wasn't by his side. He sat in alarm. "What time is it?"

"Goldenrod is here," she told him.

Beyond the window in the long dark before the dawn, fog tapped at the pane in greeting, then moved on. "Impossible. We boarded her at the vet's."

He looked at the phone's coal-black face as a faded memory played hide and seek in his brain. Déjà vu. He'd done this—whatever this was—before, but he'd never held onto it. The universe was toying with him, poking its head around corners long enough to stick out its tongue before scampering off to some new hiding place.

What was happening to him? He needed an answer, and he knew how to get it. Don't sleep. Stay awake until dawn, eyes and ears alert, a cat watching its prey, gauging the right moment to pounce, to kill, to feast. Whatever this was, it wouldn't escape this time.

There was movement in the sheets, then a feather-light hand fluttered over his shoulder. "What's wrong?" Stacey asked.

He flicked on the bedside light and dropped the phone on the bed. She was there. She was right there! And something else was there too, a lump beneath the sheets, moving slowly toward the pillows.

A pair of yellow ears surfaced from the covers, then a dark nose, then a whole furry yellow head.

Goldenrod meowed sharply, scolding them for leaving her behind.

"Oh Mark!" Stacey cried. "You didn't pack her?"

He couldn't help it. He laughed. He laughed harder than he had in an age. The more he laughed, the more he couldn't stop. He gathered both females into his arms and laughed until Stacy stared as though he'd gone full-tilt mad, and then he laughed until her resistance broke and she melted into laughter, too, and then they laughed together until all three of them flopped backwards in a lunatic tangle, barely able to breath, delirious, dying from absurdity while the cat squirmed between them but didn't seek escape.

Of course not. Goldenrod didn't want to leave. This was her doing. Mark finally got it. The fog, the dreams that weren't quite dreams, the reality that wasn't quite reality. He got it all.

Goldenrod was here. And she'd brought their magic back.

About the Author

Dale E. Lehman is an award-winning writer, veteran software developer, amateur astronomer, and bonsai artist in training. He principally writes mysteries, science fiction, and humor. In addition to his novels, his writing has appeared in *Sky & Telescope* and on Medium.com. He owns and operates the imprint Red Tales. He and his late wife Kathleen have five children, six grandchildren, and two feisty cats. At any given time, Dale is at work on several novels and short stories.

To learn more about Dale and his stories and to subscribe to his newsletter, visit https://www.DaleELehman.com.

Lightning Source UK Ltd.
Milton Keynes UK
UKHW021134211222
414263UK00017B/945